# A Dog of Many Names

## Douglas Green

Circuit Breaker Books

Circuit Breaker Books LLC
Portland, OR
www.circuitbreakerbooks.com

Cover art by Kaiden Krepela
Photography by Karman Kruschke
Book design by Vinnie Kinsella

ISBN: 978-1-953639-04-2
eISBN: 978-1-953639-05-9
LCCN: 2020925719

# A Dog of
# Many Names

# Contents

1. The Empire ................................................. 1

2. Rascal ....................................................... 13

3. Drive ......................................................... 29

4. Unknown .................................................. 49

5. Reina ........................................................ 61

6. Ilse ........................................................... 77

7. Thief ........................................................ 87

8. Catnip ...................................................... 97

9. Captive..................................................... 117

10. Artemis .................................................. 133

11. Ares ....................................................... 143

12. Athena.................................................... 151

Author's Note ............................................... 163

*She crouches. Still.*
*Her black and tan fur so camouflaged in the woods,*
*dried leaves, and dirt that you don't see her at first. But*
*once you do, her eyes grab your attention. Rounder*
*than usual, accentuated by her coloring, like sad-clown*
*mascara making even a happy face melancholy. But*
*happiness for her is only a distant memory.*

*She crouches. Still.*
*In fright. Dwarfed by the trees and bushes.*
*From her size, you'd think she was young, maybe six*
*months. But the eyes show her age and wear, more pain-*
*drenched wisdom than her two years should know.*

*She crouches. Still.*
*Her once-silky coat now dusty, mottled,*
*and torn in countless places.*

*Her brain steering all its focus on one thought:*
*Don't Trust.*

*Don't Hope. Don't let it happen again.*

*She crouches. Still.*
*Barely daring to breathe.*

# CHAPTER ONE

# The Empire

*And then, one by one, the eyes opened...*

Everything you hear about Southern California is true—stars, beaches, awful traffic—but about sixty miles east of Los Angeles lies another world. Called the Inland Empire (to convince farmers to move there long ago), it's a dusty land of factories, warehouses, and homes. A land of struggle.

For example, take Fred and Myrna Corbett. Fred's grandparents stopped here on their way from Oklahoma during the Depression. Years later, Myrna's father moved nearby for a military job after serving in Korea and met her mother one night as she sang for a touring band.

Fred and Myrna met in high school. But they were in their thirties before both suddenly realized they'd always liked each other. Next thing they knew, they were married, then pregnant, and then mourning the loss of a son who almost made it to breathing. But this only made the birth a year later of a baby girl, Angela, especially joyous. By this time, the local couch factory had closed, and Fred had started his own furniture repair business, while Myrna kept her job at the chain drugstore counter three days a week.

And now that Angela had defined them as a family, they bought a dog.

Greta was, everyone said, as perfect a German shepherd as ever had been seen. Larger than normal, with defined musculature, noble chin, and a splendid mask (the coloring on her nose and mouth), she was a natural watchdog and companion, and easily the most valuable possession—if you'd use that word—in the Corbett home.

But the Corbetts had another role for her too. Given her looks and her pedigree, they found that breeding her with José Hastings' similarly beautiful Siegfried gave them litters of pups which, after splitting the profit, brought in a welcome few thousand dollars a year. Myrna joked that, while they lived in an area called an empire, the only real imperial power around was Greta and Siegfried's progeny taking over the whole county.

Fred refused to keep Greta in a crate, except when she was nursing pups. But he did keep their eight-foot fence in good repair, to ensure no one but Siegfried would ever date their beloved debutante. Which eventually led to quite a mystery.

When Angela was almost nine, Greta was found to be pregnant again, but when she gave birth it was clear the puppies…weren't Siegfried's. All but one bore a clear resemblance to Walter, a chow-Doberman-and-more mix owned by Homer Scott down the street. But how could Walter, who was too stocky to jump over a shoebox, have managed to climb into their yard?

Fred searched the yard and found no possible way. But as he finished, he noticed muddy footprints on top of Greta's doghouse, which was just tall enough for her to have climbed onto it and pulled herself over the fence.

Pulled herself? Despite regular visits with Siegfried, she risked her life to escape to *Walter*? Fred went into the house, where Myrna was showing the newborns to Angela, and revealed his discovery. "We won't let anyone know about them till they're eight weeks old," Myrna explained. "Then they'll be so unbearably cute, no one will be able to resist them."

Angela grinned, remembering when "unbearably cute" was the term her mother would use to describe her, just before covering her tummy in loud kisses. She counted the babies out—five, six, seven, with the seventh just half the size of the others. She asked why, and Fred explained that, even inside the womb, puppies compete for food, and the smallest often comes out malnourished. "And the runts usually end up fearful, because they've been beaten up for longer than they can remember."

"Ohh!" Angela whined, and reached out to hold the tiny morsel, but Myrna reminded her not to touch them yet. Seeming to grasp the idea, though, Greta leaned over and started licking the tiny one.

And then, one by one, the eyes opened. And their personalities as well.

The cheerful brat who would bite his siblings to get more access to Greta's milk; the nurturer who spent all his awake time licking his brothers and sisters, even when they were sleeping or nursing; the explorer who had to be watched so that she wouldn't find a way out of the fenced-in kitchen ("Like mother, like daughter," Fred shook his head); the lazy sleepy boy who didn't seem to mind any treatment as long as he could remain exactly where he was; the nervous watcher, always checking around as if something bad were coming at him; the big bulky girl, shoving others all day, but with no ill will—just moving whatever was in her way. And the sad-eyed runt, pushed away by the others at every feeding time, but pulled in by Greta when she'd cry, or at the bottom of the pile at playtime, or sleeping on the outside of the tiny pack—pressing herself against whomever was available for warmth. Ironically, she was the only one who looked like a tiny version of noble Greta, while all the others looked like Walter or a mixture of the two.

AT EIGHT WEEKS, Myrna's theory proved right. All it took was posting on a website, and the phone started ringing immediately. The puppies, unable to sleep with the noise, watched to see what the furless giants were doing.

When the sixth call came in, Myrna smiled at Angela and answered, "Daisy Hill Puppy Farm!" Angela giggled, though she didn't know what her mom was referring to. But then Myrna's eyes widened suddenly. "Oh, I'm sorry, Rich. Nothing. What...?"

She looked concerned. "Today? But I'm...I'd...I'd have to bring Angela in, is that...? Okay, sure, I'll be there."

She hung up, looked at Angela, and almost said something, but thought better of it.

"What, Mommy?"

"We have to go in to work."

"Oh, Mom, I don't want to! It's boring there, and I want to stay with the..."

"I'm sorry, honey," Myrna cut her off. "It won't be for long. Something's...something's up."

They left out the back door, as sixteen eyes watched.

All the eyes were startled open two hours later, by the sound of the door unlocking and Angela asking, "What does 'got her trained like a little monkey' mean anyway? The puppies began whining, as Greta pulled them in and began cleaning them.

"What? Who said that?" Myrna asked absently, looking at her phone.

"Mr. Daniels. When we first went in. He gave me that big, loud, 'Hey, Angela! How's it going?' and I said 'I'm fine, Mr. Daniels. How are you?' and he told you that you had me trained like a little monkey."

"Oh, honey, he's just...He's not very good with people. He was actually complimenting your manners."

"Well, if he's not good with people," Angela asked while opening a bag of electric-colored candy, "why is he your boss?"

Myrna paused to think that one out. "I think because

he's good at dealing with *his* bosses. That's a good lesson to remember, dear."

The runt, getting shoved aside by the pushy pup, watched Angela give that idea some consideration for about one second, before giving up on it. "And why does he ask questions and then talk over me when I answer?"

Myrna turned to Angela. "That was awful, honey. He was wrong to do that. He asked you about your school, and then when you started to tell him about it, he turned and talked to me, completely ignoring you. I hated it."

"So why didn't you stop him?"

"Because…" Myrna winced. "Because what he was saying upset me more. I'm sorry."

Angela nodded blankly but turned to the crate. "And how are *you*, little squirrels? Did you have a good afternoon?"

"Better than ours," Myrna muttered under her breath as she opened the refrigerator.

Greta looked up from her pups and gestured a friendly lick to Angela. Two of the puppies stayed feeding, while the others came up to the bars to lick and chew her fingers. "Why do you think they smell so good, Mommy? Even their peepee smells nice."

"Oh, that's probably so we don't get mad and kick them out when they bite us with those sharp teeth."

"But they're too sweet to… *Ow!*" She pulled back her finger from the brat as he wagged his tail and headed back to his mother.

"OH, MYRNE, NO…" Fred moaned as he walked in, the watching pups able to hear his worry. "What happened?"

"I've known it was coming. Ever since they started installing those self-checkouts in the front, I've told you."

"But you've been so loyal. Who was it? Rich?"

"Of course."

Angela, holding the sleepy little one in her lap, while Greta and the other pups focused on the scent emanating from the oven, chimed in, "I don't like him, Daddy. He asked me how I liked school and I told him it was fine except that Julia Gonzales called me stupid, and Robin Walker pulls my hair, and—"

"Honey, let Mommy tell me."

Angela sat back with her mouth still open, and then looked down as the pup in her lap nuzzled her hand.

"Oh, you know, it'll be two weeks' pay—what's in the contract—and he'll write a letter of recommendation and talk me up. All 'Hey, Myrn, you know I don't make policy, right?'" Myrna said, in a good enough imitation of Rich to make Angela giggle.

Myrna and Fred smiled at her, but then nobody could think of anything to say, so the room went silent, except for the whimpering of the exploring puppy, trying as usual to open the crate's gate.

"And Mommy took me and her out for candy. And I got a—"

"'Herself and me,' honey. Or 'us,'" Fred counseled Angela, not taking his eyes off Myrna's clenched face.

"I thought the darkest chocolate I could find might help," Myrna smiled.

Angela's face soured. "I tried it. It tasted like the tar on the playground."

Fred turned to her. "You really ate the—?"

"Actually, honey, dinner's almost ready," Myrna interrupted. "Can you put him back and go wash up? Face and hands—your mouth looks like a rainbow from all those gummies."

Angela gave a silly, wide smile, with a "Yummm!" as she carefully put the squirming handful back into the crate and walked out. He sniffed at his curious siblings, curled up in a corner, and shut his eyes.

"There's something else…" Myrna said low, once the child was out of earshot. "I got a call."

"What about?"

"It's Greta," she whispered, but the sleeping mother across the room heard her name, her ears raising just slightly. "A breeder called. He saw our ad and said she's probably got only one good whelping in her left, and he'd be happy to take her where he can watch her more closely than we did, to make sure they're purebred."

"Oh, I can build our fence higher—that's no problem. Why would we—?"

"Three thousand dollars," Myrna interrupted.

Fred started to talk, but stopped, thinking. "Up front?" he finally got out.

"Cash. He says he's got buyers looking for shepherd pups, as well as wanting some for himself, and Greta's so known…"

"But I can't just give her away. That'd be like selling off you or Angie."

She took his hand in hers. "He said we'd be able to visit her all we wanted. And we're going to need the three thousand by the end of the month."

Fred sat back, his body deflating. With his mouth twisted, he thought out loud, "Well, let's check him out, anyway. To make sure he's legit."

Angela walked in. "Are you all cleaned up?" Myrna asked, opening the oven and releasing enough aroma to send all the puppies yapping.

"Clean enough for pizza!" Angela smiled.

OVER THE NEXT week, countless interested buyers came by the house to check out the puppies, till all seven were booked to be picked up on their twelve-week birthday. As it might be too difficult for Angela to watch, she was sent to her grandparents the night before the pickups, and Fred and Myrna set to glumly doling out the youths they were more attached to than they liked to admit.

First, though, they took Greta to the breeder's home, figuring it would be too cruel to make her watch her children being given away. He did seem kind and welcoming, repeating that they should come often for visits.

Then, with no time for emotions, Fred and Myrna rushed back to face the puppy-adopters. The feisty brat went to a farmer with a large field; the nurturer to a family with a child in leg braces who needed a protective companion; the explorer to a young couple who loved hiking; the sleeper to an aged couple who'd just had to put their fourteen-year-old Labrador down; the observer to a storekeeper as a watchdog; and the bulky shover to a local high school football coach, who respected the mutt's attitude toward life.

The last family finally showed up, excited to take home the funny brash nipper. "But you picked the runt. The shepherd-looking one," Fred explained.

"No, we picked the fun one. We were holding the little one, but we said we wanted the other."

"Oh, sorry, but he's gone. This one's all that's left. Would you like her?"

"Well…" the father whined, irritated. "Really, no. We wanted a fun playmate for our boys. This one's scared of her own shadow. Thanks for nothing." And they left in a huff.

Fred was still doing his best to explain to Angela, as they walked into the kitchen later, that, as expected, Greta and the other puppies had gone to other homes, and they'd put another ad out for the remaining pup. Angela didn't respond, but looked inside the crates as her father left. There was the little one, gnawing on the bars. "Are you going to be mine?" Angela whispered. "Are you my friend?"

The puppy licked her through the opening with her grey-dappled tongue and then rushed back to gnawing. Angela giggled.

Myrna yelled from the next room that it was time for bed. Angela put her finger into the cage to let the puppy chew on it, said "Goodnight, little rascal," and headed off to brush her teeth—while the puppy went back to dealing with her own, in her puppy way.

# CHAPTER TWO

# Rascal

*...wondering which, between the dog and her,*
*loved the other more...*

"**N**o, Angela, I said *now!*"

Angela sighed and pressed her nose against the warm muzzle. "It won't be long. I'll be back right after school," she whispered. The six-month-old pup, hearing her tone, gave her a big slurp across her face, and into her mouth. Angela pulled back with a "*Yucch!*" but smiled. "Be good, Rascal."

"Did I tell you why I named her Rascal, Daddy? Ms. Rubin said I'd like a book about a raccoon that had a face a lot like—"

"Yes, you told me. Let's go." He gently shoved her out the door.

There was another reason for the name, though. The Corbetts had never seen such a frightened pup. "Skittish" was the word Fred used. It was as though some person had been mean to her, but they were the only people she'd ever known. Angela hoped, now that her parents had relented and let her keep her, that maybe calling her Rascal would get some daring personality to come out.

Instead of watching through a window, as her siblings might have, Rascal walked back into her crate and curled up against the corner. To human eyes, it might have looked as if she didn't care about the girl leaving or lacked interest in what the lady might be up to. But Rascal had a different mind from most other dogs. Whereas her brothers or sisters happily ran from one room to another in play, or between outside and inside the house, she took in too much for that. She'd have to stop, or shake herself, to adjust to such a transition. Any new space, or new situation, required her to take a moment to absorb her new reality.

Fred had been mistaken when he'd commented that she might "have less than a full plate of nachos up there." Rascal smelled and heard all around her, like most dogs, but also felt weather that hadn't come yet, the vibrations of the ground beneath her, and others' sadness or anger.

This sensitivity, which made her especially reactive (had any dog ever jumped so when someone dropped a fork from the table?), also made her positive feelings overwhelming. All dogs love big, but for Rascal, love stunned. One of the adults would walk into the room, and the pup would freeze—just stare with an almost-imperceptible tremble, her ears back, her brain reeling from all her heart gushed out. And when she'd see the girl anew, the flood was such that sometimes she'd have to turn her head or walk away. And the same when the youngster would leave. The dog's whole world would shift, and she'd need to re-center, feel the loss, and get new bearings, as one does in waking from a wonderful dream into a new unwritten day.

After a few minutes, Myrna walked into the kitchen to refill her cup from the warm, gurgling machine. Rascal stood up in her crate, stretched her body, and stepped out in hopes the lady might drop a snack. But Myrna just looked down at her and sighed. "Let's get you outside, Rascal. I don't know how long it'll take to find what's out there." She opened the back door to let the puppy run out and shut it glumly, taking her coffee to her computer in the next room.

Rascal ran into the center of the yard and, as always, stopped to take it all in. Thousands and thousands of facts—smells, sounds, items in sight, even the temperature and feel of the air—sent her brain reeling. She sat, letting her nose and long ears twist and turn till she was satisfied. Then she began her walk around the yard, led by smells no human could sense, which told her now-honed mind everything that had happened there since she'd last investigated.

A couple of times, birds interrupted her by lighting on the ground. She sped over to check them out, but they disappointingly flew off. Then sometime later, the back door opened. Rascal looked up and froze—Was she being invited in? Did the lady have a treat for her?—but Myrna just looked at her sadly. "Hi, Rascal. You doing okay?" Rascal stayed still but wagged her tail at the attention and her name. Myrna broke a small smile and nodded. "You are weird," she sighed, and walked back in, shutting the door behind her.

Even though Rascal had the full run of the yard, she was always huddled still under a bush when Angela came home. But then their daily reunions would explode, Rascal's mind bursting with ecstatic electricity, as she raced around in circles, yowling with "I Missed You!" excitement, while Angela would scream in mock anger, "Rascal, you goofhead, get over here!" (Angela had explained to Rascal that her uncle had said that word when she was five, and she had never forgotten it. "Ever since, I've wanted to use it as a nickname—and since puppies don't get offended like people, I thought you wouldn't mind.")

As Angela opened the gate, Rascal ran from the bush at her, but, too excited, shot past her, jumped on the fence, ran back to her, fell on the ground, and then, just as Angela got close enough to pet her, barked, rolled over, and sprang to run in celebration again. After a couple of tries, Angela finally managed a grip on her and pulled her in for a tight hug, cooing, "Ohhh, you goofhead. My little goofhead, my little Rascal," which Rascal both loved and struggled against—the feelings merging into a sudden burst of licking and chewing on this favorite human, who always smelled way more interesting when she'd come home from those days away with her books. Then, just for a moment, the struggle stopped, as both soaked up a moment of pure joyous peace—both thinking, *It's all right. All is right. I have her again. I'll make it.*

Today's hug lasted a little longer than usual, so Rascal popped back into struggling, pawing at Angela to put her down. The moment she hit the ground, the pup bolted off, knowing the girl would chase her till she'd trade roles and run away as hard as she could, getting caught a little more quickly each time. Angela spied Rascal's favorite toy, a long-eyelashed lamb, ran to it, and began squeezing it in little jolts, knowing the squeaks would make Rascal yet more crazed, jumping and biting in the air to get her babydoll back.

Eventually, Rascal's mind relaxed, and she signaled she was finished by lying down on her chest and forepaws, panting while giving the young girl helpless eyes. Angela laughed, went inside, came out with treats for the both of them, and lay on the ground next to her. Rascal didn't know which she loved more, the girl or the treats, but her mind hadn't developed to where she'd question such a conundrum.

"And how was your day, my princess? Did you catch any butterflies?" Angela asked, pulling the chewing pup to her. "Mine stank, like always. Suzanne Dietrich has all these girls deciding they don't like me, and I can't even sit on the playground without them bugging me. And today they did it so much I walked away from them and didn't see that stupid Daniel hit a ball wrong in handball, and it hit me on the side of the head. It really hurt. He was nice about it, at least he asked if I was okay, but I—I just want to get through a day without crying, Rascal."

The dog whimpered, feeling her upset but not knowing what to do about it. She licked the pants-covered knee and turned to gnaw on the stroking hand. Angela clutched Rascal to her, and the pup, feeling too much to hold in, let out a loud yowl. Angela couldn't help but laugh, even with the tears on her cheeks. She squeezed the warm, furry body to her. "You are just…"

Suddenly she remembered. "Oh! I have something to show you, Rascal!"

She opened her backpack and pulled out a piece of paper.

"I was sitting in the classroom with Ms. Remesar before class, to keep away from Suzie, and you know I like to draw then, right? Well, I was trying to get this one anime character's face, and the eye wasn't right. But the thing is, it wasn't hers—it was yours! I didn't get the rest of you right, but do you see it?"

Angela put the paper in front of the dog, who sniffed at it and turned away—nothing to eat there—and then took her chin in her hand and compared the two faces with intense focus. "Yeah, your eyes are closer together, and your ears—they really are too big for your head, you know that? But no, you're perfect!" Angela hugged her to her chest. Rascal pulled her head back in irritation but gave her two seconds before pushing all of herself back to take some space to sit, pant, and absorb all this ecstasy.

Angela put the picture away carefully and pulled out her assignment notebook. "At least I don't have to go back there till Monday, and if I get this done now I can watch what I want tonight," Angela muttered, opening up her science text to read about animals while an actual *Canis familiaris* curled up an arm's reach away and closed her eyes to nap.

WHILE RASCAL'S MIND could in no way comprehend the concept of weekends, they were her favorite time—the grownups home more, the lady less stressed, and, best of all, more meals prepared.

"But I don't understand," Angela said while Myrna tore some lettuce. "Picnics are treated like something special, and they are fun, but anyone can eat outdoors anytime, right? So why don't we, if we like them?"

Myrna paused to think about it. "Maybe it's just because we *call* it special?" she offered.

"But that doesn't make sense," Angela answered. "If that was true, we could call any day we wanted special, and suddenly everyone would say it was."

"That's holidays, honey."

"But no, holidays are special because they always…"

Angela got quiet as her mind reached around this concept.

Rascal lay on the floor, watching their every move with the focused eyes her ancestors used to hunt deer. One slight slip of a hand, and who knew what delights might drop?

"So then, why don't we have more holidays, more special days?"

"Because every time we create a holiday, people don't go to work on that day. And people like Rich Daniels don't pay us unless we work."

"So Mr. Daniels is the one who makes most days boring?"

Myrna smiled and changed the subject. "Can you get the mayonnaise out of the refrigerator, dear?"

Angela opened the door and pulled out the large jar.

"Do you want to put it on the bread?"

"Okay." Angela took out a butter knife and began slopping dollops onto the slices. Rascal's nose went into the air, noting the sweetness.

"Oh, honey, much, much less! Just thin, like butter."

"But don't you want to taste it? I like mayonnaise."

"Sure, but that's too much! I like marmalade, but I wouldn't want that much on my toast!"

"Why not?" Angela laughed, as she put the big load back on the knife and motioned it toward her mother's face. "Is it…scaaaaaary?"

"Only when it gets on my hips!"

"Are you suuuuuure?" Angela motioned it toward her mother again. "Oops!" The clump of mayo fell *splat* on the floor.

"Oh, Angela, get a paper towel!" Angela reached to the counter, but Rascal joyously gulped it down before she grasped the roll.

"Oh, Mommy, is that bad? Should she…?"

"I don't think there's a problem, but wipe the rest up. It might upset her stomach if she has a lot of it."

"But this little bit is okay?"

"It's still cold. It's only when mayonnaise gets to room temperature that it can get dangerous."

"What happens to it?"

"If it's left out, it can go bad, and even become poisonous."

"Really?" Angela stared at the jar.

"Yes, so how about you get back to putting it on the bread before it becomes pure cyanide!" Myrna smiled.

"Okay, okay…" Angela went back to it, but smiled at Rascal licking her chops, the girl wondering which, between the dog and her, loved the other more.

AND DAYS LATER, there they were, together in the yard, happy and laughing, all petting Rascal—the man rubbing her tummy, the lady scratching her ears, while the girl ran around her in circles, kissing the top of each paw over and over as she passed. Rascal finally rolled upright, as each family member handed her their sandwich, cheering her to gobble them down, when—

The dog opened her eyes. They were gone, but…What was wrong? She was used to coming to from dreams, but something had pulled her out of this one.

The gate opened, and Myrna and Fred walked in, looking down with stern expressions. Behind them, Angela walked slowly, sobbing.

Rascal sat up to take it all in. "I think you'd better just go to your room," Fred said, looking at his feet. The girl nodded, sniffling.

Rascal walked up to her, expecting some sort of greeting, but Angela just walked into the house behind her parents. The dog waited—where did they want her?—but Angela didn't shut the door behind her.

"Come on, Rascal," the girl barely muttered. Rascal ran in, confused, and followed her to her room.

"Can you come up here?" Angela begged, flopping onto the bed. Rascal didn't need to be asked twice, curling up in a ball against the girl's chest as it throbbed. Slowly, as the dog breathed into it, the body calmed, and she started releasing the day.

"So you know how I always say the only good thing about Mondays is art class in the afternoon? It's like the one time I can just disappear into what I'm doing, painting or drawing or whatever, not like with math or grammar, or—how does a person get a zero on a geography test, anyway? But in art, Ms. Remesar won't ever tell me I'm wrong. She's even all, 'You're your own worst critic.'" Angela gulped. "But she won't say that anymore." She began sobbing again.

"And today," she said around her tears, "I thought I had the one that I'd enter into the mall contest. It was you, Rascal. I'd gotten the shape of your face good, and Daddy'd printed out a couple of photos of you I could use. And I was just beginning to really get you in there—the way you've got fear and the excitement at the same time—and then I saw it. It was those tiny eyelashes at the bottoms of your eyes, the ones you don't even notice by your sad-looking curves, on that rubbery stuff. They made you real,

Rascal, it was your sweetness, it was your goofiness, it was...

"And right then, Suzie bumped into me, hard, and spilled black paint all over you. And when I looked up, she was smiling. She'd done it on purpose! And I knew I'd never get that face so right again, and that look on her, I just—everything went blurry and I yelled and I jumped up, and I grabbed her gross face and shoved it onto the paint, hard. And all I kept yelling was 'Is this what you wanted?! Are you happy now?!'"

Just talking about it got Angela panting, as though it were happening again. She squeezed Rascal to her but let go when the puppy whimpered.

"Of course, she lied to Ms. Remesar, said it was an accident and she'd apologized. I told the truth that she was lying, but we were down the hall to Ms. Hamrick's office by then. And Suzie lied to her too, and she could tell, I saw it, but she still called both our families and sent us both home. Now I have to pay for the shirt, and Suzie's family is rich, so it'll be expensive and Mommy's out of work so Daddy has to pay for it, and he's right to be mad. Sometimes they're unfair, but not this time. It's my fault. I know it."

She started sobbing again, and Rascal licked the tears off her face. "I hate her, Rascal. I don't want to go back there, ever."

Hours passed. Sometimes Rascal would doze off, and sometimes Angela would, but only for a few minutes. Mostly she just stared up.

"I think they're asleep now, Rascal. And I know I said I wasn't hungry, but Mommy will have left me some food." She got up, walked to the kitchen, making sure to shush Rascal as she followed her, and opened the refrigerator.

Sure enough, Rascal could smell some macaroni and cheese, with a bit of turkey burger and broccoli. Angela pulled out the plate, and her elbow knocked against a jar in the door, startling the pup.

She glanced at it and grinned down at Rascal. "I'd love to frighten stupid Suzie with a glop of that, like I did Mommy." And then her face went serious. Rascal felt something change and cocked her head.

"You know," she whispered, "if I could make Suzie so sick she has to go home, the others probably will just forget about me…" She looked harder at the jar. "And you don't get in trouble if no one knows what happened to her."

She pulled it out, and started back to her room, but stopped. "Oh, that's dumb," she whispered to Rascal, who was hoping for some. "Mommy would see it's gone. And then if I put it back, it'd make us sick, too!" She opened a cupboard, found a paper cup, and put a glob from the jar into it.

Rascal started to bark. "Stop it!" Angela whispered. She clamped her hand over the puppy's mouth, shushing her when she started to whimper, and tiptoeing back to her room, holding the cup between her fingers.

Angela slept hard that night, so when Rascal woke and climbed off the bed, she didn't even stir. The pup curled up to lie on the floor but noticed something smelled interesting.

She stood up on her hind legs, pulled it down off the dresser, and licked it as empty as she could, and then chewed the waxy paper till she got the last bits.

When the sun shone in and Fred knocked on the door, the girl just rolled over and groaned, while the dog stood and shook off the night and this new stress, and walked out to see what the kitchen might offer.

Fred sat at the table, watching the noisemaking box. Rascal sniffed to see if he had anything that smelled good there, but it was either too soon or too late. She walked over to lap up water in her bowl but looked up when she heard the girl's voice yell something out in her room. She went back to her drink. Angela burst into the kitchen and grabbed her, prying her mouth open and sniffing. The confused dog pulled back but licked her hand submissively.

"Honey, what are you doing?" Fred asked.

"Oh, you know, those teeth are so sharp, just amazing!" she offered, half-looking at him to see if he'd accept it.

Angela looked at the pup intensely. Seeing nothing that wasn't normal, she hesitated, and then got up and walked back to her room, trembling at the enormity of what she'd done.

She knew they should take the dog to the vet, but that would mean telling Mom and Dad, and this idea had been so bad that even they wouldn't be able to accept it. She'd be punished, but worse, they'd forever see her as a murderer. And Rascal *seemed* okay, so she probably was?

SUZIE WASN'T AT school yet when Angela got there, so she was able to walk straight into the classroom. But as the day went on, even with Suzie glaring at her and whispering with her friends, Angela barely noticed. Every minute that went by, she was surer and surer that Rascal was down, sick, dying. Screaming in pain from what the poison was doing to her stomach.

How in the world could she have gone to school? How could she have been so selfish, so stupid, so cowardly as to not tell her parents what she'd done? Yesterday, Suzie was the worst person in the world, but today *Angela* was. She'd killed the sweetest puppy ever and hadn't even cared enough to stop it.

When the bell rang at three-twenty, Suzie and Roxanne started to step toward the door, but Angela was out before they had a chance. She ran and ran, till her feet hurt and she couldn't run more, and so just walked fast, her book bag banging against her leg the whole way. She closed her eyes and prayed, promising God she'd never do anything like this again, that she'd be good, really good, if He would just not kill Rascal. *Rascal, who would never hurt anyone, who doesn't deserve to die. Who doesn't deserve to feel any pain at all. Who is good, so good, so much better than me.*

But when she got to a few blocks from her home, she forgot her feet. She ran like she'd never run before, without breathing, it seemed. Got to her yard, shoved open the gate, and—no Rascal.

No Rascal.

*She's dead, she's a pile on my bedroom floor, wondering where I am.*

*She's dead, she's flat and still under a tree.*

*She's alive, but in horrible pain, wishing she was dead, coughing up blood and guts and...*

The eyes stared at her from under a bougainvillea.

"Rascal?"

The eyes blinked, hesitated.

"Rascal!"

The puppy bolted out, proud of having hidden so successfully, nipped her on the ankle, ran around behind her, and crouched down on her haunches, ready for more play.

"Oh, Rascal!"

This time, Rascal didn't have a chance to get away. The girl fell on her, grabbing her and holding her so tight she couldn't gasp for air.

Angela felt the pup's precious heartbeat against her—she was fine, she was playful, she was alive, and everything would be okay. *She's alive!*

Rascal whined, and Angela relaxed her grip, but held on. Another whine. Angela pulled back her head to look—no, the pup seemed just fine—so she whined back at her, mocking the sound. Rascal looked at her and whined again, but this time opening it into the beginning of a yowl. Angela laughed and made the same sound.

Rascal licked her and then opened her mouth and let loose with a shriek, letting out all the anxiety building inside her for the past day. Angela threw her head back and joined in. The two of them screamed and kissed till both gave up, exhausted.

Angela looked around the yard and the house for any vomit that might give away her sin, but if it had been there, the pup must have eaten it back up. And still, she was okay. So the mayo must not have gone bad enough.

She flopped to the ground, grabbed Rascal again, and held her to her chest. "I promise, never ever will I let something like this happen to you again. You are mine and I am yours. And nothing in my life will ever be more important than you, even for a moment, ever again. I promise you, and I promise God, and I swear, forever."

The power of what she'd said suddenly ran over her. She'd never made a lifelong vow before. She looked into the pup's not-quite-comprehending eyes, but saw the love returned.

She was suddenly a slightly older girl, something closer to a woman.

Which felt weird.

# Chapter Three

# Drive

*...something, anything, to get out of this feeling...*

The gate opened, and the dog looked up and, as usual, froze in anticipation. Her heart beating faster, she saw the girl walk in. "Hey Rascal," Angela said softly, and petted her and gave her a kiss on the nose. Rascal licked her face and got a hug back for it before Angela walked into the house. The dog rolled onto her back, facing up toward the sun to let it warm her belly, listened to the air and felt the earth, and thought about the girl. Something had changed in her, and the young dog wasn't sure why, or whether she liked it.

On the one hand, the girl was less of a playmate now. Every day she'd go straight to her books and focus on them for hours. She hardly talked at all and didn't even look at the bright noise-making machines much. At least the pup used to get stroked when she did that. Life had become kind of boring.

But on the other hand, the changes in the girl had created a nice consistency. She didn't get as sad or upset. She'd go to sleep earlier and get up before the others, which meant Rascal was let outdoors earlier.

And since dogs don't get to choose their lives, she took a breath and relaxed into what she liked about this newness, and let the oldness go, until the time it might return.

Rascal rolled over onto her side and noticed something. The gate. It was slightly open. The girl hadn't latched it behind her.

She got up, shook herself off, and cautiously walked up to smell it. Was something different about it now?

But as she sniffed, the gate wasn't interesting anymore, but the grass just outside it was, with its fresh taste. She stepped out. And then the patch of ground just past the grass grabbed her attention, where someone must have peed sometime back. And then the hard surface of the flat area, hotter than the ground, and more like rock. And then the warm vehicle there, the one the lady got into usually, hot and carrying the smells of the last places she'd gone.

Rascal looked up and took in her surroundings. She'd never been here before without humans. So much to explore, such wonders…Where to start?

Beyond the flat surface was an area where people lived whom she didn't know. She checked out their flowers, their bushes, a large tree, and then heard some sounds she wasn't used to. She followed them toward an open area, and just as she started to peer around, another, louder, sound pulled her away.

"Rascal!"

She turned back and saw the man—her man—standing by his vehicle. She hadn't even noticed it drive up.

"Wait there!" he yelled and ran across to her. He took her by her collar and led her back to their gate. "I'm glad you're okay, girl. How did this happen?"

He took her into her yard, shut the gate behind her, and opened the door to the house. "Myrna? Angela?"

"Yeah?" the two voices responded.

"Can you come out here?"

The lady and the girl came to the door. "Which one of you got home last?" Fred asked, sternly.

The two looked at each other. "I guess me, Daddy. You were already here, right, Mom?"

Myrna nodded. "I've been here since lunch. Why?"

Fred looked down at Angela. "Because Rascal was just across the street, and the gate was open. Do you know what could have happened?"

Myrna looked at the girl, whose face fell in shock. "You mean I...?"

Fred squatted down to her. "You know a dog requires you to be fully responsible, and—" But he stopped when he saw her eyes fill with tears.

"I don't believe it," she whined. "I never..."

Myrna looked down at the two of them. "I've got some-one on the phone. Angela, listen to your father about this. I have to go," she said, and stepped inside.

Angela ran straight to Rascal and took her face in her hands. "Are you all right? I'm so sorry!"

The dog, confused at what everyone was upset about, licked her hands.

Fred tried again. "You have to pay more attention to—"

"Dad? This can't happen again."

"What?"

Angela examined to the gate. "There's no reason why I should have left it open today, instead of any other. And she could have been killed! So this could happen anytime. How can we make it so it can't?"

Fred stood agape, his scolding words stuck in his throat.

"Do they make springs for gates like this? That shut behind you?"

"I...I don't know...I guess so. We can go to the hardware store this weekend and look."

"We can't tonight?"

"Hon, I have so much work to do. We just need to remember till then."

"Oh, I'll remember." Angela sniffled, looking at the gate and thinking more. "And don't they have collars that shock dogs when they walk out of their yard? To train them? I saw one once on TV."

Fred took in the changed girl in front of him. "Yes, I've heard of those too. We'll check it out."

He put his arm around her shoulders and led her into the house. Rascal watched them go, needing a moment to put all this together, but Angela turned to her. "Come on, Rascal," and so she followed them in.


RASCAL LAY ON her chin, as always at dinnertime, in her crate but poised to jump at any dropped or spilled excitement. The girl sat quietly, probably too focused to slip, but the grownups were animatedly talking, so there was hope.

"I do have one interview tomorrow at a phone store, but if that doesn't come through, I'm not finding anything else listed."

"Well, I hope it does, and if I can win this account too, we can relax a bit."

"What is it, Daddy?" Angela asked, not looking up.

"Well," Fred turned to her, surprised, "a new offshoot of the community college is taking five rooms of an office building, and wants to have a regular system to repair their furniture, since the students constantly wear it all down. If I can snag that contract, we might be able to keep the house."

Myrna gave Fred a look. He caught it and glanced at Angela, but she hadn't reacted. Rascal shifted her weight, unsure what was happening.

"Oh, but we'll be okay either way. I got the boxes from the printers. The folders look great, the papers look professional." He laughed. "I even paid them extra to proofread it all, to make sure my bad spelling doesn't turn off the educators." He looked for a reaction but didn't see any. Rascal thumped her tail, hoping changing their focus might result in a treat.

"It's just like making furniture." He turned to Angela. "I have to put them together in the right way, no mistakes, so no one falls on their butt, right?"

She gave him the smile he wanted but put her fork down. "I'm good. Can I be excused?"

"You don't want dessert?" Myrna asked. "I got ice cream."

"Oh, that's okay, thanks. I need to get to work. And I didn't get enough exercise at recess today."

"Ange." Fred sat back, choosing his words carefully. "Is everything...okay?"

"What's wrong, Dad?"

"Nothing at all, you're just...You're just being great. I just wonder..."

Angela shrugged. "I'm concerned about more responsible things now."

"And that's terrific, hon. I mean, you do your chores without asking; your mom told me you'd finished last summer's reading a month early..."

"I think your father's trying to say he's proud of you." Myrna looked back and forth between the two of them, smiling hopefully. Rascal whined softly.

"Okay...?" Angela waited for what was coming.

"She's even playing sports at recess instead of sitting alone, you know." Myrna smiled even larger at Fred.

"Well, yeah, but that's just 'cause that's the best way to keep Suzie and her stupid friends away."

"And what are you reading now?" Myrna added. "Besides homework?"

Angela shifted nervously in her seat, "Um...Ms. Rubin gave me a list of some books. I'm starting *A Wrinkle in Time* now, maybe *Little Women* after?"

Fred looked between them, again unable to find words. "I'm just not that C-student I used to be anymore," Angela said, and left.

"I wonder if she's happy," Fred said to Myrna, as Angela carried her books to her room. "She doesn't seem to smile as much."

"She hardly cries, either," Myrna answered, getting the ice cream out. "Maybe it's a pre-tween thing. At least her appetite isn't exploding."

"Oh, I wish she'd eat more. She's skinny as a fencepost."

Myrna smiled at him. "Enjoy it while it lasts, Papa. Her daddy's-little-girl days are numbered."

He winced. "And that's not cheap, either."

"You've heard that, have you?"

"Yep."

Myrna picked up a pile of bills from the counter. "So I've been going over these, and if we can just get through the end of the year, we might be able to keep the house and the car."

Fred frowned at one bill. "Well, hopefully we'll at least never have to replace a designer shirt again for some snotty little rich…"

"Shhh," she whispered with a smirk. "If she can't say that word, we can't."

They both mouthed it anyway.

The dog rolled over and let out a groan, relaxing into the disappointment of another dinner with no spills, as the adults talked about boring things.

SOMETHING MADE RASCAL want to sleep in the kitchen that night, but her tail thumped at the sound of the girl's approach. As always.

She loved early mornings. Entering the day by falling into a hug from her favorite smell, caressed by her favorite hands—hands that petted and scratched her, hands she loved to lick.

And she was so warm as Angela put her into her lap. "You are perfect," Angela whispered to her. "You're the only perfect one." Rascal chewed on her wrist as Angela rubbed her tummy.

"And what are your plans for today? To chase some very naughty squirrels? Oh, thank you!"

Rascal leaped up and licked her nose, biting her just slightly. "Oh yes, I do think that's a good idea, too! Lots of kissing."

They looked into each other's eyes. Each wishing she could comprehend this loved other.

Overcome, Angela pulled Rascal to her neck, "Oh, goofhead!"

As always, Rascal lasted a second in that full embrace, before pushing the body away with a whine, and then looking at her and giving another.

"No, we can't howl till they're up. But let's get you outside; your bladder can only hold so much!" Angela opened the lock and let her out and watched the pup gallop in joyous clumsiness. And as her eyes saddened, she responsibly shut the door.

THE INLAND EMPIRE avoids extreme humidity, but its sun and heat can accomplish the same madness. Everyone feels the world is conspiring against them, not grasping that the blinding brightness, the tired air, and the searing burn that comes from touching anything in the sun's rays have nothing to do with them. Lots of car accidents. Lots of power blowouts. Lots of fights.

Rascal had just worked her way from the midday sun to under a cool bush, when the larger vehicle drove up and she saw her lady get out. She came in through the gate, latched it, and turned into the house without even a pat. Rascal followed her in and lay on the floor, looking up at her.

Myrna sat at the kitchen table, pulled her phone out of her purse, and looked at it. "Okay, what?" she muttered as she pressed it.

A thinned version of Fred's voice came out. "Hey, guessing you're in your interview. Just sending you kisses. Knock 'em out!" Rascal sensed the man's forced enthusiasm, and the disappointment emanating from the lady.

"Hey, Myrna!" came a female voice. "Hope you're good. A bunch of us are getting together for a girls' night after work. We'd love to get you there. Aww, it's been forever! We're going to—" She shut the phone off and put it down.

She stood up and opened the refrigerator. Rascal stayed still, but with her eyes zeroed in. The lady pulled out a plate of what they'd eaten last night and sniffed it. But instead of shutting the door, she paused and took out a tall green bottle, pulled the top off with a soft pop sound, and picked up a glass. She started to pour but stopped. "No..." she whispered to herself, and poured the glass out into the sink. "No." She filled it with water and took a drink from it.

Leaving the food on the counter, she walked back to the adults' bedroom and flopped onto the bed. Wanting to be near her, Rascal followed, but stopped at the door, sensing too much unpleasantness coming off of her.

The dog lay back in the hallway, looking up at the lady, till she heard her breathing grow heavy in sleep. Quietly, she stood up and walked away, making sure not to noisily shake off the feelings till she walked out the back door.

By mid-afternoon, even under the bush was hot, and the pup was panting. Too uptight for a hiding game, she jumped up at the sound of the girl's footsteps and ran to leap on her, knocking her down onto her backpack. "Ow! Stop it, Rascal!" Angela whined, and pushed the dusty pup away. Rascal, liking this new game, jumped back in and nipped her hand. "*Ow!* Stop that!" Angela barked as she reactively punched Rascal with her fist.

Rascal yelped—the girl had never done that before; what was wrong?

Angela looked up in shock. "Oh, Rascal, I'm..." She sighed in frustration. "Oh, come on inside." She let the dog into the house.

She opened the refrigerator, grabbed some grapes, and turned to the confused face. "I'd rather watch some stupid TV show, but...I'll feel bad if I do." She sat at the kitchen table and opened a book while the dog sat hopefully. "I don't think you'd like these," the girl muttered, rubbing her eyes. She read more. "But this story doesn't go any-where—he just looks for these sheep and...Why do they assign this? It's so boring!" After a minute more, she exhaled and flipped the pages. "I've had it. I'll blow the quiz, but who cares…"

Rascal pushed an old sock of hers into Angela's lap. Angela took hold of it, but as Rascal gave a first pull, she let it go, giving the dog a disappointing win.

She picked up another book and opened it. Rascal ran up with the sock again, hoping her timing would be better now, but Angela softly pushed her away. "I'm sorry, Rascal, just not now. I…"

She looked down at the textbook again. Rascal felt a disturbance, a sense of danger, she'd never felt from the girl before, and stepped back, as Angela gritted her teeth and squeezed her eyes shut. "*I…can't take it!*" she screamed, throwing the book at the wall and frightening the dog out of the room.

"Angela? Are you all right?" Myrna's sleepy voice came from the hallway.

"Sorry, Mom, I just dropped something," Angela lied, embarrassed.

Awakened and drawn back into the kitchen later by the smells of cooking, Rascal protected herself by squeezing into her crate. The lady delicately set plates on the table. "Fred? Angela!" she called without looking up.

"Coming," came both voices, followed by the two walking in.

Rascal looked through the bars and nervously studied her family, her pack, for any sign. Feeling unsafe here was new to her, and she didn't like it.

Each sat down silently. Each irritable, the silence as loud as yelling.

"So, how was school, honey?" Myrna offered.

"Nothing special."

"What are you doing in science these days?"

"Parts of flowers."

"Oh," Fred offered, "that's pretty interesting, how they're so different from us."

"They're plants, Dad."

"I know. I'm just trying to make conversation. Is that so bad?"

"Sorry."

"Apology accepted."

Myrna winced and tried to catch his eye, but he went on.

"Well, I had a productive day. I'm all prepared for to-morrow's meeting."

"That's wonderful, honey," Myrna said, meaning it. Rascal's tail thumped.

"And how about you, Myrne? Any luck with that inter-view?" Fred asked, trying too hard to sound casual.

Myrna rolled her eyes. "They'd hired some kid before I even got there."

"What?!"

"Tell me about it. Even the boy was embarrassed."

"Well I hope you opened up a can of whoop on them."

"Oh, I just walked out. What's the point?"

Fred's face tightened. "Well, what then? Did you talk with anyone else?"

Rascal whimpered too softly for anyone to hear and

pushed back to the wall. Angela looked down at the napkin in her lap.

"With who, Fred?" Myrna asked through tightened lips. "Oh, excuse me, *whom?*"

"I don't *know*, Myrna. But it's your job to go looking, not mine. I'm busy trying to save the one job we've got!"

"Damn it, Fred, stop acting like I'm not!" Myrna finally let out. "You try going through this! It's been over a year!"

"Oh, believe me, I know!"

The pup started chewing her feet in nervousness. Angela, avoiding their faces, reached over. Rascal lightly licked her finger in appreciation, still not sure what to do with all the tension she couldn't help absorbing.

"Remember, I go through the books. I'm the one who knows just how much money we have, and how much we don't!"

"What's that supposed to mean?" Myrna blurted out. "Who puts all the bills into just the order you want so you can look at them?"

Rascal suddenly sat up, pushing the hand back, and let out a howl, hoping the girl would join in with her. But she just scowled down at her and hissed "Ssshhh!" Rascal whimpered and walked out of the room, her tail between her legs, and down the hall, where she could still hear the man's voice rise to a higher pitch. "And I suppose that takes all day, five days a week?"

"Stop it!" Angela yelled. "Would you two just *shut up?!*"

The dog tensed. Something very bad had happened.

"Angela! Don't you *ever* talk to us that way!" Fred snapped.

"It's not her fault," Myrna groaned. "Would you want to sit at this table? Fred, I'm done searching. I'll take any work, but I can't go through more of this."

"You're quitting?" Fred slapped the table so hard the dog heard the plates rattle. "Myrna, I'm doing everything to keep this house. Do you understand?!"

"What part do you think I don't? Stop acting like I'm some sort of idiot!"

Angela ran out of the kitchen. The dog watched her approach.

"Angela! It's not you. No one's—" Fred tried, but Angela slammed her bedroom door behind her. The dog backed farther down the hall.

"Fred, I—" Myrna started, but Fred bolted up and left for the living room.

"Thanks a lot!" Myrna blurted, and started cleaning the table as noisily as she could.

"Just leave it," Fred yelled. "I'll eat mine later." He was answered by the roar of the garbage disposal clogging with food.

The dog's tension was too much to take. She scratched her chin hard, bumping against something that looked chewy. She sniffed at it and took it into her mouth. It helped. She rolled onto her side and chewed more.

After a minute, Fred's voice burst out, "Angela! Come on out. Your mother's dessert'll be ready." Waited. No sound.

"Angela?!" Nothing.

"Angela, do you want me to come in there?!"

"Fred, please, just let her be," Myrna moaned from the kitchen.

"No, you know what, she can't disrespect you like this!" He stormed up the hall to slam his hand on Angela's door, when something caught the corner of his eye, and he turned.

There, on the floor of his bedroom, their bedroom, hunched Rascal, nervously chewing the promotion folders. The ones that were still left. Though she must have already ripped up twenty.

"*Nooo!*" he screamed. "You stupid—! Get the hell out of here!" He grabbed the dog by the scruff of the neck and jerked her up into the air. Terrified, she screamed, and, in a flash of panic, tried to bite his hand, making him squeeze her more tightly.

Angela burst out of her room, saw the sight and froze, unable to breathe. Myrna ran out of the kitchen. "Fred! What are you—" But he pushed past her, opened the back door, and threw the terrified pup down into the yard.

Rascal, her world imploding, pulled herself into a protective ball and stared at the doorway, as the man blinked at what he'd done, and suddenly broke out crying. "I just can't take it," he choked. "Why would that dog do that?!"

"Because she's stupid," Angela uttered, coldly. Myrna and Fred looked up to see her standing in the door to the hall. "Stupid, like you." She turned and walked back to her room, this time closing the door in deliberate control.

Myrna took a deep breath and let it out slowly. "Fred, I'm sorry. I'm so very, very sorry." He took her in his arms and held her to him, where she could feel the tear streaks on his rough face.

"You've got no reason to be," he said softly. "You've been great. This is just me." He held her more. "There'll be an all-night printer somewhere. I'll go find out where," he whispered gruffly, and walked away.

Rascal, looking up from the ground, sensed what the lady was experiencing—a fear that everything in her life could disappear. A need to change something, anything, to get out of this feeling. And a memory, of another time she'd shut herself down. A little death of self. An ancient tool for survival, a cold one. To find control. To protect her family.

Myrna's voice called out, "I'm going out for a drive. I'll be back in a bit."

"'Kay," Rascal heard Fred through the window. She wagged hopefully at his calmer voice. "Try not to be too long. I might have a long trip to a printer."

But Myrna had already stepped out of the house.

GLAD TO BE in the car, away from the home that today made no sense, Rascal pressed her nose on the window, till Myrna noticed it. "Oh, here, have some air," she said as she rolled the window down.

She kept driving east while Rascal sniffed away at every scent they passed. "Oh, wait!" Myrna realized, pulled Rascal back in, and put the window back up. "I don't want you memorizing all the smells."

Rascal sighed and curled up on the seat. Her mind still wishing it could make sense of the day.

Myrna kept staring forward. She spoke words as if to Rascal, but really to herself, hearing how they sounded.

"You're going to be fine. You're an animal. It's wrong to keep you penned in. And now you're afraid of Fred, so you'll be happier this way. Out here you can chew up everything you want. And you can hunt and find squirrels and mice and birds. It's a way better life."

Rascal gave a sigh, relaxing into her seat.

"And really, it was your job to connect with Angela, and she doesn't feel anything for you. You used to play with her, but now I don't even see that. You're not a people dog. You're really meant for this."

She crossed a bridge over a shallow river. Under her breath, she muttered, "Even a top tracking dog would have trouble finding her way back if they can't find the bridge, right?"

She turned to the right at the first large road. "We'll get a dog again. We'll get a really good one like Greta. She was more appropriate for the family. You're more one for the country."

As the dog dozed off, the lady drove further down the road, and then pulled over to the side. The dog came to.

"Okay, Rascal. Here you go. Time for a new life."

Myrna got out and opened the trunk. Rascal's ears

shot up as the lady spilled a small bag of dry dog food out onto the ground. "And here's to make it better," she smiled as she poured liquid over it, liquid whose smell was recognizable from dinner.

She opened the door, and Rascal jumped out, sniffed, shook herself to adjust to this newness, and started lapping up the food off the ground.

"Bye-bye, little girl. Good luck." As her eyes teared up, Myrna patted the puppy's head, and started back into her car.

"Oh, wait." She reached down to Rascal's collar and twisted off her tags. Rascal whined and strained against the little strangling, but didn't stop eating. "Keep the collar, so they'll know you have a family. Had."

She climbed back in, shut the door, and paused, with the engine running.

She inhaled and looked in the rearview mirror. Rascal was still eating. She shifted into drive and started forward.

She drove about twenty feet, before making a U-turn back toward the highway. As she passed the food, Rascal wasn't there. But then she saw the pup, running after her down the street. She accelerated hard, enough for the puppy to give up. Then slowed down when she knew she was far enough away.


SHE BEGAN TALKING again, this time in rehearsal. "She must've gotten out. Was the gate open? She'll be back. Unless she's having too much fun."

She thought more. "You didn't like her that much anyway. You didn't play with her. We'll get another dog when you're older and more responsible. Plus, she didn't like me or your dad much, either."

Suddenly, her stomach turned. "Oh no." She hit the brakes and made another U-turn back.

"Angela'll think you ran away because of Fred. And the only way to tell her would be to—" She sped up. "And does she really not care about you?"

She braked when she saw the stains of gravy by the road. She pulled over, got out, and called Rascal. And called.

Nothing.


MAYBE IT WAS okay. Maybe she'd already gone off hunting and was having a good time. Maybe it really was for the best.

But something inside Myrna froze yet colder. A little like strength and a little like not quite herself. And a little like eleven years ago when…but best not to think about that.

She drove on, keeping rehearsing what to tell Angela, and wondering how long that frozen part would be there. And how it would change her.

# Chapter Four

# Unknown

*But still the road pulled her in...*

The dog looked up, confused, as the lady shut the car door. She'd never left food on the ground this way, and hardly ever did she give her the wonderful-smelling foods the humans ate. The little girl, sure, but not the lady.

The pup had gone out in the car before. Sometimes for fun trips with the family, and other times to that cold sterile place that smelled of chemicals, where people poked her with needles and reached into her uncomfortable places. But the lady always put her back in the car when she left. So she kept eating, knowing the lady must just be doing something in the front seat. Plus, lapping the tasty food up felt comforting, relaxing her nervousness.

But the car started moving. It pulled forward and then turned around. What?! The lady didn't remember she was out here! The dog ran from the food so she could catch up and get back in, barking loudly.

But once the car turned around, it sped away. The dog ran as hard as she could, but the bright lights on the back just got smaller and the roaring sound of the engine just got softer.

And then it wasn't there at all.

She kept running and running, following the smell of the exhaust. But no, it was nothing but gone. She stopped and stood still in the middle of the street, panting. While her body gasped for air, her open mouth looking like a smile, growing terror filled her eyes, as her brain stifled in shock.

And incomprehension. This just didn't happen. The lady had never forgotten her before. Was it possible?

Was the lady angry at her? The man was, but he seemed mad at everyone.

But there wasn't time for that. For now, she just had to…she couldn't think what. Oh, sure—to get back home. But how? And could she quiet her fear enough to get there? She lay on the ground and let the dizziness in her go its way. But when the fear got too strong, she stood up to make some decision.

She put her nose into the air. Did anything smell familiar? No, not yet. But she was pretty sure the car had been going the direction they'd come from, so she shook herself and started walking that way.

She made it about a minute before lights came toward her. Oh good, the lady remembered! She stood in the middle of the road, ready to get in. But the lights got brighter and brighter, and the roar louder and louder, and didn't seem to be slowing down at all. Suddenly the oncoming machine yelled out a huge terrifying sound, making her dash off the road as it marauded past her.

It wasn't their car. It was larger. And faster. It might even have run into her if she hadn't gotten away.

Looking carefully to make sure it wasn't coming back, she stepped back into the middle of the road, and started walking the lady's direction again. After a while, the road began to get brighter, and louder, and another sound blared at her from behind, and she ran off to the other side. Was that her?

The smaller vehicle shot past. The dog watched it go and felt her heart start to stab. This was so alone. She was used to feeling lonely when the humans left her at home during the day, or in her crate, but this was different. She didn't know this place at all.

Why didn't the lady hurry up and come back? Another car whooshed by, but this time, since she was still off the road, it didn't threaten her, or blare that noise. This was good. She'd stay off the pavement but keep walking toward her home till her car found her.

She walked on and on, till she came to where her road didn't go any farther, and she'd have to head either left or right. She sat and whined. How to decide? But then, a deep instinct inside her told her—turn left. She did, and walked on, always trying to stay out of the lights of any machines.

After a long way in the dark, trying to ignore the smells and sounds from away, she smelled water, and walked to it. She put her foot in, but it moved, frightening her.

She hesitated, but took another step in. The flow pushed against her legs. But she felt strong enough for it. She took one more step, and her foot fell—suddenly no ground underneath—and she tumbled over.

The rushing pushed her body sideways and splashed over her head. She scrambled her feet around till she got a foothold back on the side, and pulled herself up, and out of the water, knowing she wouldn't try that again.

She shook off as much as she could and looked around. A way lay overhead, some sort of road over the water. She stepped to the start of it and stepped in to cross over.

In the distance, a sound came to her. Was that—could that be the lady's voice?

Suddenly, out of nowhere, another bright-eyed giant rushed at her, screaming that sound. But this time, there was no side of the road to hide on. And there wasn't time to climb up the side. So she pulled herself into the tiniest ball she could and squeezed against the little wall. The monster zoomed past her so closely she could feel the heat of its wheels.

The moment it was gone, she looked ahead. There'd be nowhere to go if another one came. It was too scary. And maybe that had been the lady calling her. Besides, she was starting to get hungry, and there was that food waiting where the lady had left her.

She walked and walked, turning where she'd turned, staying off the road where she could, till she found the spot.

But there was no food.

She sniffed around. She could tell where it had been, but it was all gone. Had the lady come back and cleaned it up, the way she did in the house? Or maybe there was someone else out here?

She had never known predators. She'd had only the humans of her home, and her mother and siblings, and the birds she'd chase for fun in the yard. But another voice of old, very old, instinct suddenly told her to feel afraid. Whoever ate this food might be around still, and not friendly.

She saw a clump of bushes, and thought that might be a good place to sit, to wait for the lady to come back. The ground was hard and dusty, but she felt a little safer there than out by the road, as she curled up as hidden as she could. She sat and watched for coming cars, but hardly any more came now.

After a while, she let herself lie down on her chest. And her mind began grasping something, something awful. That maybe this was how things were now. And all the comfort and love she'd felt, and counted on, was somehow gone.

And worse than that, it was on purpose—she'd been taken away and left. She wasn't wanted. They disliked her now. She had failed. There was nothing she could do. Nothing was safe. And if nothing was safe, nothing made sense.

And this overwhelmed her, to where, slowly, with every exhale a slight whimper, her eyes closed, and the world went away.

LOOKING DOWNWARD, SHE saw the girl walk into the yard. Just like any other afternoon, but the girl hadn't expected her to jump from the tree above and tackle her to the ground, licking her face and making her laugh uncontrollably. The girl got herself up and ran across the grass, where the pup caught her again, knocking her against the fence. But just as the dog jumped onto her, she turned to her with terror on her face, and cried out "No!" The pup held her breath as the word grew into a giant horrified scream.

The dog's eyes opened as the biggest vehicle yet tore her from slumber, shaking the ground and letting out an ear-piercing screech as it slowed down. She dashed behind the bush so it wouldn't see her. But it was gone quickly.

Meanwhile, the day had begun. With light in the sky, she could see around her. And she'd never seen anything like it.

Except for the road, all around her was open landscape. No houses or fences or strip malls, just hills and grasses. Not as frightening now. She stood up, stretched, shook herself, and sniffed to see what might be interesting.

As the smells pulled her away from the road, she felt a worry that the lady might come by, but other voices inside her said to keep sniffing. To discover about this place—if there was anything fun. And maybe find some…

That was what was missing. She hadn't eaten much last night, and no one was feeding her this morning, either. What was she supposed to do about eating?

She licked at the ground when she found something that smelled like it might be good, but it never tasted right, so she went on.

And then, as she went farther and farther from the road, she started to feel better. She was not finding what she was after, but those voices inside were saying something was right about this, something old, that she'd never felt before. Something strangely...wonderful.

And suddenly, she began to run. Didn't really decide to, just her legs taking her. Running just because she could, because she had never run where there was no limit before, no edge, no one calling her back.

She stopped. No one calling her back.

That deep pain that she'd had in the night started again, and with it, the whimper. She looked around at the endless horizon, and once more it didn't feel exciting at all, but instead a view of growing dread, that being alone wasn't going to end, that she had been abandoned, thrown away, unwanted. And that never again would she have her crate, her people, her food or water bowl...

And with that thought—it wasn't just hunger. She needed water, and there wasn't any. Hadn't been any since she went to sleep, since before that. The lady hadn't left her any when she dumped the food out. And here she'd run so far, following the lady all the way to the...

There *was* water. She just needed to get back to it again and not step in. She wandered back to the road, knowing her senses would track to where she'd come from, and turned once again toward the way the lady had driven off.

The sun was warming up, making her pant to keep herself cool, which only made her thirstier. But just as she got to wondering if she'd turned wrong, she came upon the moving water again. Keeping her back feet out, she cautiously stepped to it to drink.

It wasn't clear like the water she got at home. This was dirty, with plastic and metal junk on the sides, but she didn't care. She lapped and lapped at it, hoping not just to quench her thirst, but to fill that deep painful hole in her heart. Since this was all she had.

Exhausted, she walked over to a shady tree and plopped down onto the ground. And wondered where to go now. A more frantic whine started inside her, as sadness gave way to the return of pure fear. A faster whine. Her eyes scanned all around her—no food, no help, forever. She wanted to yell out, but stopped herself, that ancient voice saying not to call trouble in.

Instead, her stomach squeezed in on the water, and turned in sharp pain—pain from the fear, the sadness, the all alone—till it finally gave way and all the water she had drunk pushed up and out of her mouth. Instinctively, she looked down and lapped up all that had come out, not caring that it was mixed with the dirt. Anything inside her helped a little.

She shook herself and stepped away from the wet area, when her eye caught something in the distance. A group of birds had flown down and were walking around in the grass. Without thinking, she leaped toward them. But they heard her and flew out of her reach at once. She yelped and jumped helplessly. One member of their group, sassy or stupid, flew back down to the ground, but shot up into the air before the pup could reach her.

And again that old voice inside her spoke—now saying to hide. But why? Was someone scary around? And where? She found a small bush she could get behind but still see around, and lay down behind it.

Nothing happened except an occasional insect flying by. She waited and waited. And slowly fell asleep again.

Now she was a young whelp, whining as her siblings pushed her away from her mother, till the giant nurturing nose shoved them aside and allowed her to feed on her milk. Milk so warm, so sweet, so filling of her tiny tummy.

HER EYES OPENED—SHE'D slept through another night, to find a squirrel walking a few yards away. This was what the voice must have wanted, for her to let it get near. She pulled herself up and lunged at it.

The squirrel, shocked at the sudden attack, ran as fast as it could, but the attacker came closer and closer. But he turned suddenly, knowing the bigger animal could never spin as quickly, and made it to a tree in time.

The pup barked in anger at her target getting away. But she stopped and decided to just sit and wait for the pest to come back down.

She lay there for what seemed forever, as the sun moved across the leaves and branches, knowing the little creature had to move down eventually, just trying to outwait him.

In a flash, behind her, she heard a flapping. She turned and saw two small birds fighting in the grasses. She jumped at them as they began to fly, chomping her mouth so close she caught dust off one's tailfeathers. She gave a sigh and turned to go back to the tree—just in time to see the squirrel reach the ground and start away.

She bounded after it as quickly as she could, finding it in herself to accelerate faster, but just as she got close, it turned swiftly again, and left her scrambling as it escaped easily back to the tree and up. It turned and barked at her.

Furious, she barked back wildly. Hunger was giving way to hatred—she *had* to catch that twerp. Suddenly it was *his* fault she was miserable, alone, starving. And catching him could solve all those problems.

She lay down, staring up at the branch where she knew he was. This time, she wouldn't lose focus. She'd keep on him till he had to come down.

More time went by. The tree swayed in a breeze, the sun kept moving till all was darkness, but she kept her nose focused on the tree, her ears occasionally picking up a rustle in the leaves.

And then, it was her last night in the house again. The man was yelling, the lady and the girl were both upset, and she wanted nothing to do with this scene. She walked out of the kitchen and into the dark front room. Suddenly, lights came at her out of the darkness, blinding and noisy.

She jumped out of the way, as the giant roared by her and into the kitchen.

She ran behind it and looked in, and stopped in shock: Everything was gone. The table, the stove, the counters, the people. Just the room was there, desolate and empty.

She stepped in to sniff it out, when the machine turned around and headed back—for her! It was too late to get out of the way—it was aiming straight at her, screaming, and...

She awoke. Day beginning again. She looked up into the tree but couldn't see enough to tell if her tormentor was still in the branches. She sniffed at the trunk—sure enough, he'd been there. But had he come down or gone up? She whined—there was no way to know.

But there was nowhere else to go, so she lay back down to wait in hope.

And her eyes opened again. She looked into the tree, and although the sun was still low, flashes of light blinked in the branches. She rubbed her eyes on her forepaws and looked again. No—no more lights. She looked into the distance. Were those birds, or something else floating across the sky? She got up to check them out, when she realized another dog was standing next to her.

It was her mother, looking down on her with warmth. The pup licked at her, knowing she was now saved. But for some reason, her tongue wouldn't make contact with the great body. The sensation of licking at air made her stomach nauseous. She started to vomit, but nothing came out, just dry heaves.

She walked away from the tree, the squirrel now seeming unimportant. It was hard to even walk a straight line, the world around her all in flashes.

She didn't know why, but she found herself heading toward the road.

No, not the road—one of those things would come along and hit her.

But still the road pulled her in. Step by step, almost circular in her direction, she kept heading toward it. Not even hearing the engine sounds roaring by her.

She meant to stand, was trying to, but found herself lying on the ground. Her legs too weak to lift her up to shake. Or to pull her from the roaring sound approaching her, or the high screaming next to her head.

Or the sound of a door opening, or a man's voice as he approached her.

She couldn't even open her eyes as he picked her up and put her inside.

CHAPTER FIVE

# Reina

*...confused but excited—first the rat and now him...*

S he awoke, some.

She'd never felt this way before. Still dizzy, she had a blurred memory of eating some food. It seemed like a dream, but she could taste the residue of it in her mouth. But something else was wrong. Not the way it should be. She opened her bleary eyes and slowly realized—she was lying on a couch, which was against the rules.

She pulled herself off it and landed on the floor, making her head hurt. She started to sniff around. Where was she—a strange couch, a small rug, a table—when suddenly a little boy walked into the room and yelled too loudly.

"¡Mami! ¡Papi!" he burst out in delight. "¡La perrita esta despierta!" A man and another boy, a little bigger, stepped in. The little one ran to the dog, who pulled back in fear. A woman's head looked in and chided "¡Toni!" in a voice that stopped him and pulled him back to give the pup more space.

As she cautiously resumed sniffing, the father went into the kitchen, brought out some bits of chicken, and handed them to the boys. "Con cuidad," the father warned. "Despacito, hijos."

The boys approached slowly, with care, but the pup, who had never learned to fear people, especially any with food, cantered up and licked their hands clean. The bigger one smiled up at the man while the younger giggled.

The dog sat in front of the family and checked out their faces. Was anyone else going to bring her something to eat? The man put his hand out and she sniffed it, licking the residue off his fingers. "¿Con permiso?" he asked, and gently put his hands around her chest. She didn't struggle, so he lifted her and held her in his arm. "¡Ay! ¡Mira que dulce!" the woman beamed. The dog looked toward her and gave a small nervous lick. The people seemed harmless, but up here she was as helpless as when her siblings shoved her away from food.

The boys took her outside to play, and she shook off the strangeness in the familiar air. She needed a tree-stop something awful, but then turned and looked at them and shook again. She couldn't quite understand what was going on, but they acted friendly, like the girl. The big one threw a ball. Thinking it might be food, she chased after it, but disappointed at its uninteresting flavor, left it and walked back to them. The older one explained to the other that they'd have to train her to fetch—her owners must not have played that with her.

Still exhausted from days of not eating, she flopped to the ground and looked around. She saw they had a big vehicle, maybe what they brought her here in. Maybe they would take her back to her home? She walked up to it and whined. But the boys called her inside and motioned to her to climb back onto the couch. She looked at each of them, confused, but they didn't seem to mind, so she pulled herself onto it and relaxed. Not closing her eyes yet—just looking at these new humans, her tail thumping hopefully, trying to figure if she was as safe as things appeared.

The bigger boy pointed out how regal she looked sitting up there. "¡Que sí!" the woman agreed. "¡Como una reina!" The whole family laughed, and the little one declaimed, "¡Eso es! ¡Perrita, vamos a nombrarte Reina!" and ran up to pet her. His excitement frightened her, but he didn't seem angry, so she gave him a tentative lick.

Everyone here sounded a little different from the humans at home, but she could understand much from the tones of their voices, just as she had there, and the way they kept saying "Reina" to her made her figure that sound had something to do with her.

"Dejala dormir, mijo," the woman said, and the young boy dutifully got up and, with a kiss on the dog's tail, left her on the couch. She looked around the room, noticing how different it was from her home. Smaller, with scents that revealed age—things here were old, with history in them. The couch didn't smell of chemicals the way the other one did, and had scratches and holes in the fabric.

There was something comforting here. But even so, she was awfully tired. She curled up and took a deep breath, and was out cold in seconds.

A few hours later, the boys took her out again, this time with the man. He explained to them that it was essential they start teaching her now, so she didn't develop bad habits. He spoke to her very directly: "Sientate." She looked at him, wondering if they were going to run around more. "Sientate." She cocked her head. He gently reached over and pushed her butt to the ground. She licked his arm and stood back up. "No. Sientate." He pushed her butt to the ground again, this time patting her on the head, "¡Sí, Reina!"

Wait, she thought. Is this like "Sit?"

He stood her up again. "Sientate," and she plopped her butt onto the ground. "¡Sí!" all three yelled. She jumped up on the larger boy in excitement—these guys were fun—and he gave her a little hug.

Suddenly they heard a blaring horn and turned. Two men sat in an old vehicle. "¡Alfonso! ¡Tenemos trabajo!"

The father smiled and walked up to them. "¿Para mí o la familia?"

"Sólo tú, es muy pequeño," one of the men in the car grinned.

"Tonto," muttered the father. "Continúan, chicos." He gestured to the pup and joined his friends.


Over the next couple of days, Reina's mind swam as it accustomed itself to this new world. The house was smaller than the home she'd always lived in—all four humans slept in one room, on mattresses on the floor. The building itself had holes in it, like the couch. And she learned about these new people. The mother cooked every day in the kitchen—everything smelling good, not just about half of it like in the earlier house. No one had the regular schedules everyone had there, either; sometimes they'd all go off to do something that made them tired and sweaty, and sometimes only one or two would—but if anyone went, the man did.

This family had more friends than the others, too. Every night they'd have people in, or they'd take her to other small houses. There, she had to be on alert—she'd never known rooms so crowded, with getting stepped on so likely. And lots of little children who might grab her tail, and adults whose breath smelled of chemicals who were clumsy or accidentally rough with her. And sometimes other dogs—smaller, who irritatingly barked at her and ran away to hide when she'd snap at them. But as long as she was careful, she delighted in everyone welcoming her with petting and generous dropping of food.

AND SLOWLY, AS weeks passed, Reina found herself connecting more and more to these new people—the adults just as caring and providing as the other couple, the older boy a bit distant, but she could feel his understanding, and the younger clumsily madly in love with her just as she was with him.

And meanwhile, she thought less about the other house. When a vehicle went by outside, she hardly ever wondered now if it was the lady. When she heard children's laughter, she didn't look out as often to see if one was the little girl. She didn't focus on how that other couple were getting along now, but on how these boys annoyed each other and sometimes one would punch the other—teaching her to keep her distance when their voices would rise. Her heart still hurt, but now it just seemed part of her, not asking a question all the time.

And her dreams, once always about that world, now included the other places she'd known—the roadside and this home. Often chasing a squirrel up a tree, chased by both the families, none able to catch her.

THE SOUND OF giggling made her eyes open. There was the older boy, watching her forepaws running and her mouth snarling. She gave a sigh—as that delightful world lifted away.

He put the loop of a tied rope over her head and slapped his thigh to tell her to follow him, and they walked outside.

The boy yawned while she sniffed around and peed on a wall and then found some more interesting smells. He pulled on the rope, but she stiffened her legs to keep herself there.

"Reina, come on! That's enough. We gotta get to the store and back by five."

She had noticed before that, when he was alone with her, he spoke in a way that sounded more like her earlier family. But, comforting as that was, she had also learned she couldn't fully trust people who spoke like that.

"I'm glad *you* think this is fun. I wish I could send you to do it by yourself. You'd love that, wouldn't you? Me and Toni, we was watching this show on how they train dogs for blind people. So if you can lead one of us to a place, why can't you just go yourself? Maybe Mami could pin a note to your collar with some money, and then you could bring everything home? It'd be too big and heavy, but if you pulled a grocery cart, maybe you could do it?"

She walked on ahead, pulling at the rope. There was something she liked about this boy. He wasn't as affectionate as his brother, but that meant he hadn't hurt her with tight hugs so much, and his calm energy was soothing.

"You'd probably like it, too. I wish I was like you, could get happy about just having something to do. I hate this. I hate this walk, I hate what I'm doing, I hate this stupid town, I hate that Toni doesn't have to do anything, I hate Toni most. Come *on*, you don't need to sniff everything!"

He pulled her harder, lifting her forepaws off the ground. This was what was great about these walks—anytime she got dragged away from one enticing smell, there'd be another just ahead.

"I'm not like you, and I'm sure not like my family. I don't know what they want, don't know why we even came here. They're okay with this life, but it's *caca*. Once I can, I'm getting out of here. I'm going to L.A. That's where something can happen. That's where I can get a car, get the girls to look at me, not like here where I'm like I don't exist."

They reached the store, and he tied her to a fence and pulled out his shopping list. She looked up at him to see if he was going to abandon her there. He leaned over and scratched her head, and she gave his arm a lick. He thought a second, sat down next to her, and looked her in the eye.

"Hey, Reina, what if I took you there? No one would mess with me if I had you. I mean, you look like you could be scary, and they wouldn't know. What if…Reina, what if you and I ran away?! I'd leave them a note; it'd be okay, I'd call and let them know when I got there. And then someday me and you, we'd drive back and pick them up and take them there. Well, maybe we leave Toni here!"

He laughed and gave her head a happy shuffle with his hand. She lay on the ground, happy to check out the scenery, while he walked into the store, studying the list.

THE NEXT MORNING, Reina was chasing the boys in a field, when suddenly they were standing in front of her…but in the house, waking her, with the little one's usual desperate hugs. She gave a little whine at the confusion.

The mother came in, hurrying the boys up and telling them to leave the dog alone. She went into the kitchen and looked for whatever food they could take. The father walked in, dressed in the work clothes Reina loved the smell of the most, and hurrying the boys up as well. They complained about being rushed, but just then there was a blare outside. "¡Vámonos, mijos! ¿Mari?"

The mother came in with a bag. "No es mucho, pero…"

"Es okay," he smiled, as he opened the door.

The young boy turned around to look at the pup they were preparing to leave on the couch. "¿Papi? ¿Podemos traer a Reina?"

The man looked at her and thought a second. "Sí. Está bien. Hay muchos ratones allí."

Excited that they might get to see her hunt, the older boy grabbed the rope they used as a leash, and the younger squealed and gave her a hug. The four people and the dog ran out and climbed into the back of an old pickup truck—the younger boy and Reina needing help getting up that high.

Reina had never been in a vehicle without a roof before, so was instantly excited, frightened, and curious, all at the same time, and ran around as far as the rope on her collar would let her. "¡No, Reina! ¡Sientate! ¡Es un truck!" yelled the littlest, but the man shushed him. The boy gave him a perplexed look, wondering how this could be okay, but just then they turned a corner quickly, sending Reina tumbling tummy over tail. Hearing everyone laugh, she curled up in a corner to protect herself from that happening again.

The drive was long, but Reina found the fresh air helped her stomach feel not quite as queasy as in cars. They arrived at a street with a number of houses, parking in front of a large structure of frames of wood. Other men dressed like the father stood around, laughing or sucking on the strange-smelling sticks that made smoke. The man explained to the boys that they had to be careful and stay focused on whatever he told them to do. And that if everyone worked really hard today, they might end up with enough money to get ice cream afterward.

He then jumped out and joined the other men, to discuss their plans. The woman took the boys and Reina and gave them all treats. She explained to the younger boy that his main job would be watching Reina and keeping her safe, but that it would be fine to let her chase anything she wanted, as long as they stayed away from anyone carrying wood or tools. The older boy grinned at Reina and mouthed, "She doesn't say those things to me anymore, because I'm an adult now!"

"¡Cristian!" the man yelled. The older brother looked to his mother, who nodded, and ran to join his dad. The woman asked the other boy if he was sure he understood. He nodded, and she walked off to the others.

The younger one took Reina by the jowls and smiled at her, making her smile back at him. He told her how this was going to be the best day ever, with both of them helping and being useful, while catching lots of cool animals. Once he was sure she understood, he took the rope off her neck and let her go.

She pulled away, just far enough that he couldn't grab her face anymore, but happily sniffed near him. She squatted to pee after a couple of seconds, not needing much inspiration. But while she did, her nose caught something a couple of feet away, and she let it lead her down a pathway, tail excitedly wagging. He followed, excited.

The other boy's voice rang out, "¡Toni! ¡Tráeme la caja de herramientas!" Toni looked up, annoyed. He sighed and walked glumly to the truck, dug out his dad's heavy toolbox, and pulled it down. He winced at the weight as he carried it to the ladder by where Cris sat above, looking very important. Toni gave him a glance and set the toolbox on the ground. "¡Toni! ¡Toni!" Cris yelled, angrily, but Toni walked away, not turning to see Cris having to climb the six steps down to pick it up.

"¿Reina?" the boy called. She wasn't where she'd been, but after a few seconds, he saw her, sniffing more frantically around a tree. "¡Reina, ven aquí!" he ordered. Reina ignored him. "¡Reina! ¡Ahorita!" he demanded. Still no reaction. He stomped to her and put the rope over her head again. She didn't react till he pulled her away from the smells, getting a frustrated whine out of her. "Okay," he told her, but ordered that from now on she needed to obey him the first time. He gave her a swat on her butt to make sure she remembered, but now that she had returned to the scent, she didn't notice that, either.

Suddenly her ears shot up. A scuffle in some bushes near her. She dove, and out popped a large mouse. She'd never seen one before, but instinct kicked in, and she swooped at it. It turned fast, just as the squirrels had. But this was so much smaller! She bore down on it and almost had it, when it dove into a tiny hole beneath a tree root. She slid in the dirt, almost falling, and barked at it in fury, but it refused to come back out.

The boy laughed in glee. "¡Te voy a ayudar, Reina!" he exclaimed, and pulled on the root while she dug at the hole. "¡Vaya, Reina, vaya!" he exclaimed. But dig as she might, whining wildly, the ground was too hard for her paws to get much traction in the soil.

He looked around for a rock and started chipping away at the hole. With every try, he got up a few clumps of hard dirt, but while Reina appreciated the help, she could tell the mouse was long gone. She gave a last disappointed whimper, looked up at him, and sat. He smiled, wiped the sweat off his forehead, and gave her a hug. She licked his ear. He hugged tighter.

Suddenly, she pulled out of his arms. "¿Qué?" he asked, but her feet were scrambling. A mouse—or was it something bigger—was digging into some grasses a few feet away. Reina dove into them, and, while he screamed and jumped in excitement, scrambled about till she slammed her foot down. She had it. Her heart almost beating out of her chest, she leaned down and snatched it into her mouth. But before she could even bite down, it turned and bit her on the side of her cheek. She yelped, giving it just the time it needed to jump out of her mouth and run off—while she stood straight, stunned with surprise. She'd had it under her paw, she'd had it in her mouth, and it had bitten her. Three new experiences in a few seconds. She shook all over, but still her brain spun.

He ran up to her and took her face in his hands, to look at the bite. It didn't look like much.

"Buenos días, muchacho," came a voice from behind him. The boy turned, and Reina pulled back and barked in surprise, having been too focused to hear any footsteps. A tall man in a work shirt and a tie smiled at the child. "¿Cómo está?"

"Bien, ¿y usted?" the boy got out, politely.

"Muy bien, gracias. ¿Cómo te llamas?"

"Antonio."

"Bueno, Antonio. ¿Y está tu familia aqui?"

Toni didn't like this, but he didn't know what he could do. He'd heard of scary people who might be mean, but he'd also learned never to disobey an adult, as that brought the scary in people out. Still, maybe he could get away with just a little lie. "No, solamente yo. Yo y mi perrita."

"Veo." The man smiled, as he approached. Toni looked around, nervous, as the man put his hand on his shoulder. "¿Y cómo se llama tu perrita?"

"Reina," Toni said, his voice starting to break in fear.

"Ay, que bonita. Venga, Reina," the man gestured. Reina stepped forward but felt the boy's fear and didn't come all the way. Toni started toward her, but the man grabbed his shoulder and held him back.

"No, señor, permítame…" Toni whined as he pulled.

"Hey, Mister!" came the voice Toni feared most. He gasped and turned to see Cris approaching. "What are you doing?"

"Do you know this boy?" The man turned to him.

"Yeah, he's my brother. You want to take your hands off him, or should I call the cops?"

The man smiled, let go of Toni, and pulled out a badge. "Don't worry—I'm not going to hurt your brother. But, Antonio…¿por qué me mentiste?"

"No le digas nada a él," Cris snapped at Toni. "Vámonos."

Toni obeyed and followed his brother. "No, stop, boys," the man said nicely.

"¡Corre!" Cris yelled, and both boys broke into a run.

"*Stop!*" the man yelled and chased after them. Reina barked and chased him, confused but excited—first the rat and now him—and got in front of him. "Oh for God's sake!" he snapped and kicked her away.

Another man ran up, dressed like the first, pulled out a can and sprayed it into her face. She yelped as it burned her eyes and fell down to wipe at them.

The mother, Marisol, pounding nails, heard the commotion and turned. "Ay, Dios mío, no..." she gasped. "¡Alfonso! *¡Alfonso!*"

The father, working a power saw, heard nothing, till his friend tapped his shoulder. He let go of the saw's trigger and turned to his wife's scream. He then saw their sons, now grabbed by the police, and then, knowing the worst had happened, closed his eyes in a quick prayer, and started down the ladder.

REINA, STILL ON the ground, kept wiping at her eyes enough to see as the men put her family into their car and shut the door. She barked and ran to it, jumping up. The young boy, sobbing, saw her and turned to ask his mother something, but her answer wasn't good. He looked back to the dog and put his hand up on the window. She jumped up to lick it as the car started and pulled away.

Pulled away!

Her mind splintered—this couldn't be happening again! Her heart screaming in horror, she barked more, and chased the car a block. But just as before, her fastest wasn't fast enough. And once she turned down one street and couldn't see the car, she knew it was useless.

But wait. A glimmer of hope: maybe they'd come back? They didn't last time, but maybe now? She sat and waited, panting.

But no. The same.

After what seemed forever, she walked over and flopped on the side of the road. She licked her paws and wiped her eyes more. She kept looking and listening. But the day went on, with no sign. A couple of times a car would slow and a person would stick their head out and call her over, but they might be mean like that man, so she turned away, and they drove off.

As the night began, she thought it best to give up. Besides, maybe the family would be back at the place with the mice. So she turned back that way.

But as she rounded a corner, in the distance, she heard something she hadn't heard since she was a puppy. The cheerful barking of dogs, a group of them. They didn't sound dangerous, so she turned and headed their way to check them out. After all, where there were dogs, there must be food.

Carefully, shyly, she approached a house surrounded by a large fence. The barking grew louder. There must be a whole family of dogs there, she thought. She walked up and looked in.

The dogs saw her and came running at her. She stepped back—were they barking out of anger, or were they friendly? She barked back—just so they'd know she wasn't an easy mark. They barked more.

A door opened. "What's going on here?" a voice yelled. And then: "Oh. Well, hello there. Where did you come from?" And the gate began to open.

# Chapter Six

# Ilse

*It just was, as it had always been...*

She stepped into the yard, her tail between her legs. The scents of countless dogs, past and present, slammed her senses—like nothing she'd experienced since living with her siblings.

"Come on, you're fine." The man spoke with a rough but soft voice. The other dogs kept their distance. He carefully reached around her. "Nothing to worry about," he said and felt all over her body, sensitively but not like a hug.

"Seem all right," he muttered to her. "You fixed?" He felt her belly, and she rolled onto her back, showing the stranger she'd be submissive. He smiled. "Well, we'll get you some confidence later; let's get you something to eat now." He opened the door to his house.

She stepped in, too unsure to shake, but her nose went straight to the bowls on the floor. He filled one halfway with kibble, and she went to work on it. He watched her, interested, while she ate. "Good girl, good girl."

Once she finished, he opened the door again to send her outside. Not sure if this was a good idea, she hesitated, but he pushed her from behind. "Go on, meet your new family."

The others were on her at once. Her tail had never tucked so far before as they sniffed at her. One, a puppy, nipped at her feet, trying to get her to play, but she was more focused on the other three. A male, large, just seemed interested in how she smelled, while another, medium-framed but muscular, kept trying to butt him out of the way. The female was the concern, though. About her own size, the dog held back, walking in circles but watching her out of the side of her eye. This looked to be trouble.

She crouched down and rolled over, showing her belly. The female growled, but just as she approached, the man came out again with a leash. "Come on, you—we're going to check you out. They said they can see you if we come in right away." He turned on the female. "Acacia, get back!" and kicked at her. She jumped away. He slipped the leash over the frightened stranger's head and pulled her out through the gate.

He led her into the back seat of an old truck, and she curled up into the fragrant vinyl as he took off. She studied him from behind. He was built kind of like that male dog in the yard, not tall but loaded with tensed muscles. He had long hair hanging from the front of his face, and he carried the acrid smell of those sticks the good-smelling man's friends would light on fire, as well as that bitter hot drink humans like in the mornings. He didn't switch on the noisemaking buttons as most drivers would. There was something solid about him, like he knew what he was doing, but she wasn't sure whether that was good or not.

He turned into a driveway and parked the truck. He opened the door. "Come on, get out," he said and led her through a door. She could smell animals, but also chemicals, and heard whining and barking in the near distance. What was this? One of those poking places?

He went up to a counter, spoke with a woman, and started filling out some papers. She asked him a question, and he looked down at the dog.

"I dunno, something German?"

"Brünnhilde?" the receptionist asked with a grin.

"What the hell? No, something shorter."

"Ilse?" she asked.

"What's that? That lion?"

"No, it's spelled different. Not sure what it means. Let me look." She looked at the screen on her desk. "German version of Elizabeth. I-L-S-E."

He thought. "Okay, that'll do. Ilse. Yeah that's good. Thanks." He finished the papers and then sat down. The dog sat by him, figuring that was what everyone wanted.

A woman entered, carrying a box. Something about it smelled interesting, when suddenly it meowed. The dog's ears perked up—what was it? The man jerked back on her leash. "Leave it alone," he muttered.

The woman smiled at her, placed the box on the counter, and turned to them. "Is she friendly?"

"Not sure yet," the man offered. "Stray. Just got her."

The woman reached her hand out gently. The pup sniffed it and gave it a cautious lick. "Oh, she's an angel," she cooed.

"We'll see." The man gave a slight grin.

"They're so amazing," she began in a tinkling voice. "A dog is miraculously born wanting to love. Human babies need love, to receive it, and over time, learn to want to please, and eventually give real love. But puppies just get it from the get-go."

The man looked down at the pup but didn't respond. She continued. "Kitties are mysterious, otherworldly. And that keeps them safe. But dogs are so trainable, so eager to please, that they can become anything. Look at her. You can see, she's had some of her joy crushed out. But still, she's got a chance."

The woman behind the counter said the man's name, and he took the dog with him and followed her back, nodding to the cat lady.

"Another, Neville?" the veterinarian asked.

"Showed up outside my fence. Wasn't going to send her off."

"Good man," she continued, as she felt around the dog's jowls. And to the pup, whispered, "It's all right, girl, just checking."

"Name's Ilse, but she just got it. Any signs of anything?"

"She seems healthy. We'll take some blood, of course. Any idea if she's had her shots?"

"Nope. She fixed yet?"

The doctor felt her belly. "Doesn't seem to be. Want to?"

"Damn," Neville muttered. "There goes a few hundred. But, yeah, better. Don't need a litter of mutt puppies to feed. And between Colt and Needles, the odds aren't good."

"Cheaper to do the two of them, you know."

"Yeah, but no. Want 'em to feel...themselves, you know."

She gave a half smile.

"Well, maybe you don't know, but there's a feeling..."

"It's okay, Nev."

ABOUT AN HOUR later, after too much being stuck and poked, Ilse followed the hairy-faced man out into the truck. She'd liked the veterinarian, though not the shots, and hated when they sprayed something up her nose. But she felt more comfortable once she got in the back seat again and was beginning to like the feel of it. And this man wasn't like the ones she'd been with before, but he smelled like his dogs, so he must be all right.

He arrived back at his house and opened the car door. "Come on. Back in." The dogs ran up barking as he approached the gate. "Colt! Get back!" he chided as he opened it and led her in ahead of him. "Now, Needles, get along."

He walked into the house and shut the door. She turned to them, again lowering herself to the ground and showing her belly with her tail between her legs. Colt, the big furry one, and Needles, with the muscles, both sniffed her over, while the puppy, whom the man never called by any name, tried to lick her belly till she turned away.

Satisfied with the information they'd gleaned, the two adult males sauntered off, while the puppy kept jumping in at her, trying to get her to play. But she knew more was coming.

Once the two males left, sure enough, the female lunged in at her. The puppy jumped away as Ilse screamed in fright. She knew better than to fight back, but the dog didn't seem as interested in setting her alpha female position as in hurting her. Ilse turned away, but the dog bit her ear, hard. She yelped, as the door flew open, hitting the side of the house, "'*Cacia!* Get off her!"

The man grabbed a long stick from inside that had a metal wire loop at the end, got the loop over the female's head, and jerked her back from Ilse, making her yelp in frustrated pain, and then grabbed her by the collar and dragged her into the house. He slammed the door behind them.

Ilse curled up in a corner and licked the spots she could reach. Colt and Needles walked up to check her out, and the puppy climbed on her to lick the wound on her ear. Scared of all of them, Ilse shivered and whimpered.

Eventually they left her to herself, and she drifted off to sleep.

Up into the yard came the lady from her first home, and the two boys from the second. They called her to come with them, but she hesitated—they'd left her alone before; would they do it again? They walked up to her, and the younger boy hugged and nuzzled her, but then bit her ear, hard.

Ilse yelped, waking herself up. No people. Just the yard, and a fence keeping her from getting out. Or could she?

She pulled herself up and limped, checking the fence. The other dogs lay on the ground watching, knowing what she was doing and its futility.

For the next days, she managed to avoid the female, or maybe Acacia just thought it better not to attack her. Ilse worked to make it clear she intended no threat to her position as queen of the yard. And to emphasize the point, she wouldn't even socialize with the others, so as not to arouse any jealousy.

Meanwhile, the man would take her on little leashed walks, working to teach her some words. But unlike at the last house, he didn't offer her any treats for getting orders right—he just jerked on the choke collar or made an irritating clicking sound with a little device when she got them wrong. But maybe, if she did everything right, he wouldn't hurt her worse, she hoped.

And, more quickly than before, she adapted, to become more one with this place. Her new life might lack the affection and companionship she'd known at her other homes, but she was eating regularly and had some sort of safety from the world, so she was able to shift her mind to an acceptance, that this was the way things had always been and would always be.

Still, one morning, she woke agitated. Nothing was wrong exactly, but she had an anxious feeling. She paced by the fence for an hour, giving a snarl to the other dogs if they came near her. When the man came out to feed them and train her, she jumped up on him the way she would have on the girl. But he shoved her to the ground and scolded her, getting a confused yelp out of her.

Her training didn't go well that day, either. She seemed to have forgotten all he had taught her about heeling and down-staying, and his jerking and clicking only made her more scattered, with no improvement.

He pulled her back into the yard, annoyed, and stomped into the house, shutting the door. She wanted in; she wanted comfort and quiet and to feel surrounded, as her ancestors always had in dens. Besides, for some reason, she was feeling nauseous.

She dozed, waking to find the three adults sniffing at her. She pulled back in fear, but Acacia walked away—it was Colt and Needles who stood by. She sat up and began to give one of her disturbed howls, when Needles jumped onto her. She pulled away and barked. The hair went up along her back as she snarled. He stepped back, but once she turned, he came at her again.

Colt flew at them. She backed away in fear—was he going to attack her too?—but she wasn't the target. Colt hit Needles like a wall, sending the smaller dog tumbling. Needles jumped up, ready to fight, but Colt hit him again. Clearly, Colt had learned that Needles was too quick and strong to fight the usual way; he just used his size and weight. But this time, Needles didn't hesitate. He lunged at Colt's neck. Colt yelped and rolled, taking Needles down, and shoved his paw onto the smaller dog's throat, growling over him. He waited for Needles to stop writhing, and carefully lifted his paw. Needles started to move, and Colt barked loudly, into his face.

And that ended the battle for supremacy. Needles slowly crawled out from under him and slunk off to the far corner of the yard.

Colt walked over to Ilse and gave her a little lick on the ear. She was surprised that she suddenly felt like licking him back as well. But then she curled up in fear again—what might this big dog do?—and he left her alone.

Something was changing in her. She couldn't make sense of it and didn't try. But it led her to prance around the yard, taking more note of Colt.

And then, without her even thinking about it, about an hour later, she invited him to climb on top of her. She'd never felt anything quite like this before, but that old voice, that instinct voice, said she'd felt it thousands of times. It wasn't that it felt good, as much as that it felt deeply right. The way playing felt, or cuddling up with one of her favorite people, or chasing birds. It didn't make her want to do it again, or not to. It just *was*, as it had always been.

She curled up, exhausted, and closed her eyes. Immediately, Needles jumped on her again. But this time she turned on him furiously, barking and biting and dodging as she never had before. In seconds, Colt was in the middle of it as well, grabbing Needles by the throat to get him off.

Then, just as Colt seemed to have control, Acacia leaped onto Ilse, seeing a chance to finish the job from before. She grabbed Ilse's front paw and bit down. Ilse screamed, but

Colt was too busy with Needles to help. Ilse tried to get her teeth somewhere on Acacia, but the jealous cur had planned this one out and kept herself just out of reach, till she found a moment and jumped onto Ilse's throat, sinking her teeth in. Ilse howled in pain and terror as the puppy barked, bouncing in excitement, not knowing what to do or who to side with.

Suddenly there was a screech outside, the gate flew open, and Neville ran in, yelling words Ilse had never heard. He grabbed a thick stick on the ground and hit Acacia till she yelped and ran across the yard. He gave one hit to Ilse as well, just for having been in the fight. She whimpered in pain and curled up on the ground, before he turned to Colt and Needles. He hit them harder, over and over, but neither would give up, so he jumped into the middle to pull them apart, yelling in pain when one accidentally bit his knee.

Ilse saw her chance. Forgetting them, she ran as fast as she could to the gate, and out. She was halfway down the street before she heard the hairy-faced man yell her name. Knowing he'd be able to outrun her with his truck, she ran into a yard, ducked behind a house, and headed into some trees.

Her paw hurt horribly, but she kept running. She didn't know where she was going, but somewhere out there, no one was going to bite her or hit her, and that was all she cared about for now.

# CHAPTER SEVEN

# Thief

*Her senses exploded—she was in*
*an echo chamber of smells…*

She ran as fast as she could. Blinded by confusion, her pain blocked by fear and excitement, she had no idea where she was going, but her feet kept racing, across street after street, through yards, over and under bushes.

After blocks and blocks, she found a hiding place in some trees, and stopped to pant. She looked back, her ears twitching, but didn't hear anyone coming. She cautiously lay down, her chest still heaving.

All she could think of was to stay there. She'd been fed enough not to worry about eating, and couldn't even feel wanting anything now. If she could stay still, maybe she'd be safe. If she could stay still forever.

SHE DIDN'T REMEMBER when she'd slept so long. It was the next day before she awoke. She stood up, feeling more pain in her back and legs than before, but still managed to shake herself down.

And here she was again.

No home to go to, no food, no water. She began to explore, trying to remember anything she'd learned out here the last time, and wondering if perhaps some slow animal would be willing to be consumed. She walked out into the open area, crouched, and looked around. Nothing.

She heard some birds chattering, but they were up in trees, far too far away.

Finally, one lit down to check something out on the ground near her. She waited till it turned its face away and charged toward it, but it flew up before her first paw hit. She watched it soar into the sky, yelling obscenities back at her.

She started to walk back, but a thought hit her. She turned and sniffed where the bird had been. There were some little seeds on the pavement, almost too small to see. Normally she'd ignore them, but she licked them up and swallowed them. Not enough to feel even a momentary satisfaction, but maybe she could find more.

She sniffed around, till she heard a car approach. Scared of who it might be, she ran to hide behind a tree. The car stopped at its corner, but then drove on. She realized that almost all of them did that, so as long as she could hide for a few seconds, any danger of mean people coming out of them would go away.

This awareness relaxing her, she continued checking the place out, finding enough seeds to take away only the worst of the hunger pains.

As night fell, she went back to her spot in the trees, and lay down, not sure of what to hope for. But she fell asleep in disappointment, as the area stayed quiet.

After a fitful night with dreams of everyone she loved or trusted leaving her, she awoke, and wondered if being quiet might bring a different sort of small animal near. She stayed out of sight of the cars and waited. A couple of birds alit, but she knew they were too far for her to reach.

Her stomach began to squeeze—would she be able to find something to eat, ever?

A car lurched to a screeching stop at the corner. She turned. Could they see her? The window rolled down. She tensed. The sound of yelling and crying from inside told her she was right to hide. She backed away, just in case.

"No, we're not! And I'm not kidding around. I told you this would happen if you didn't stop it!" yelled the driver, as she reached around and threw a paper bag out the window. A scream and crying came from inside. The window rolled up and the car drove off.

The dog watched it go, glad she wasn't in it. She waited a bit, frightened of the anger, but her curiosity grew too strong, and she stepped out to investigate the bag.

As she got closer, her interest grew. It smelled of a mixture of salty and fatty, just what she'd like. She stuck her nose in. The inside was warm. Foods wrapped in paper, but since the paper was greasy, she ate it as well as the long, thin, salty, crispy pieces, and, most wonderfully, the cooked meat with sauces and vegetables and cheese and bread. Clearly, she had found a good place to stay.

She stepped back into her hiding place and waited. Over the rest of the day, many cars stopped at the corner, some with their windows down, some with loud music coming out. But no others threw any food out for her. She tried to figure if she'd done something different to make that happen, but couldn't think of what it might be.

But one thought arose: Humans, if they didn't see her, often had food, and she could get it. Each of the houses she'd lived in had places where food went after the people had eaten all they wanted. She was kept out from them, but did those rules apply now? She certainly felt no loyalty to anyone out here.

But how could she get into people's kitchens?

She fell asleep and dreamed of the bag she'd found. Even things in it she'd have turned her nose up at before, like those sour, wet vegetable chips on the meat.

She awoke. The sky was dark still. And those dreams only made her hungrier.

She got up and shook her sleep off, and walked a few blocks toward the houses, wondering how to get in without facing the meanness of the people in charge there. Could there be a way?

She sneaked past the cars parked outside one of the homes and looked at the door. She cocked her head, trying to figure it out.

As she studied it, a scent came to her. Very slight. She turned and followed it, to a large plastic box. One of a group of them, along the fence. There was something inside it, something that didn't smell all that good, but much better than hunger.

But how to get inside?

She stood up against the box on her hind legs, but it was too tall, and gave way slightly, tipping against the fence, making her slide down.

She whined and backed up. Could she get higher up if she ran to jump on it? Might as well give it a shot.

She ran and jumped, trying to catch the top of it with her paws. She caught it slightly but felt the whole box tip—not against the fence, but the other way, right on top of her. She yelped and jumped back as it hit the ground with a loud bang.

She looked around and ran. Someone was sure to come after her for this, but where to hide? She saw some bushes around the house and crawled inside them.

And then, nothing happened.

No noise, no lights, nothing.

Which meant...

She stepped out slowly, sniffing around, her eyes peeled. Still nothing. She slinked up to the fallen container and put her head in. Her senses exploded—she was in an echo chamber of smells. Old chicken on bones, some molding cheese, foil bowls with sauces still in them, paper towels filled with juices that had spilled...This had to be the best meal ever, and she'd gotten it herself, without any human help. There was one thing missing—that love that she'd felt when the girl or the mother or even the hairy-faced man gave her dinner—but in place of that feeling, she was safe. She wasn't locked in a house or a yard, and no one could leave her. No one could say no. No one...

As long as she stayed unseen.

She remembered to get away, before anyone showed up. She pulled herself out of the barrel, and, after looking around to make sure no one was there, pranced back to the park she'd made her home.

THIS NIGHT HER dreams were beautiful and happy, though she kept awakening with stomach pains. But these jabs were so much better than the hunger, even the one time she vomited, that she remained content. And when she woke in the day, a new sensation trembled all through her. A touch of confidence.

She could live this way. She could find these boxes outside homes—at least that one person's—and never need anyone again, unless one of her nice families came back to get her.

The morning air was brisk and cheering. She waited to make herself visible till there were no cars around, and then stepped out. She walked down the street till she came to a house. Sure enough, it had some of those same barrels outside it.

She walked up and sniffed them. One smelled of plants only, and one just had the acrid scent of big people's breath after parties. But the last smelled almost as good as the one from the previous night. She jumped onto it and knocked it against the wall of the house.

Instantly, a noise came. People, scrambling. She hid. The door to the house opened and a woman stepped out yelling. She saw the barrel on the ground, cursed, stomped over to it, and lifted it up, putting everything that had fallen out back in, muttering harsh words. Then she turned around and saw the dog in the bushes.

"Get outta here, you stupid mutt!" she yelled. The message was clear enough. She turned and ran out of the yard, faster when the woman started throwing bottles from the other barrel.

She stopped at the end of the block and looked back. If she could show the woman how nice she was…could she be one of those humans who'd be nice back to her? The woman yelled and heaved another bottle, which landed on the street and shattered into pieces, sending her running further.

Once out of sight, she headed back to the park. Another lesson learned—only go to the barrels at night, and be ready to run if a person comes out.


AND WITH THIS, she perfected her routine: sleep through the day in her den in the park, and find trash barrels at night. She even found herself eating more than she ever had before, her body craving as much of the findings as she could get down. Sometimes, sure, she'd get into one and find no food. And other times her noise would make someone turn on a light and yell, or come outside. But even in those cases, she had learned how to handle herself and get to safety.

Something was happening to her brain as well. Before this, she'd always been about someone else—her mother, or a human family, or the man and his pack. But this was an older feeling, about herself. Her own wants and needs were all she answered to. But still, it felt like a connection to something else. Not quite her litter, but somehow to that voice she'd heard before, and to all dogs. Thousands of years of stealing from humans. Timeless and infinite in its stretch. But also simply and uniquely her.

She figured out that going to the same house repeatedly would be a problem, so she gave herself a simple rule of heading down different streets each night. Sometimes the first house would have so much garbage she would just head home after that barrel, while other nights it might take four or five blocks to achieve a meal.

It was one of those nights, many streets away from home, when she was sniffing at least the fifteenth set of receptacles, that a small truck drove up and turned down the next driveway. She waited, still, watching.

A man in a uniform got out and walked up to the front door. It opened and an older woman stepped out.

"Oh, Officer! I'm so glad you were able to come so quickly."

"Yes, ma'am, I was only two blocks away when the call came in. That was very lucky, extremely. Did you see the dog?"

"No, but I could hear it shoving my barrels around. And lots of my neighbors have been getting ransacked."

"Yes, we've had a number of complaints. I'll check it out."

"Oh, thank you very much. And you be careful—you never know; it might have rabies or distemper or something."

"I appreciate your concern, ma'am, but yes, we're very careful. Have a good night."

He went back to his car and started to back out of the driveway. The dog stepped back, making sure to get behind the barrels to keep unseen—and accidentally pushed one of them into another, making it fall over.

A light turned from his car to the row of barrels. She crouched down, trying not to breathe loudly.

"Come on out, doggy. It'll be all right," the man crooned. "Come on…"

"Excuse me, sir?" the woman called from next door.

"Yes ma'am?" he turned back to her.

"Would you like a coat? It's quite chilly out tonight."

The man smiled, and walked toward her, explaining that he was doing just fine.

The dog, seeing her chance, crept out from the barrels and toward a row of bushes. She put her nose in, when a furious raspy barking spat right at her face. She stepped back, her ears up. What was this?

She hadn't even noticed the smell of them before. But this group of something she'd never seen was next to her face. The large one barked again.

The dog turned and looked behind her. The man was heading back. She could face these angry things or face him. Making her choice, she growled low at them, and stepped all the way in.

The big one bit her on the nose. She barked in pain,

making them all jump in fear and scurry out toward the driveway.

The man yelled and ran back toward his car. "It's not a dog, ma'am! It's raccoons! A whole family of them!"

The mother and her kits ran as quickly as they could across the yard. The man followed them with his spotlight, seeing what bushes they ran into, and climbed into his car.

The dog licked her paws and gently touched her nose with the saliva. The bite wasn't deep, but it hurt hard.

She kept this up, barely moving, till the man drove off down the street and disappeared.

The moon was bright and full, which gave her more visibility. But this night, as happened every seven or so, all the barrels she found were empty. She kept looking, in hopes of something showing up, but now it was getting so late the sky was lightening.

Figuring it wasn't safe to head all the way back to her den, she crossed the street and found an area of trees to sleep for the night. Even as she dozed off, her dreams weren't about her people, but about finding food, thieving, scavenging, being wild.

Which made it odd when, from deep in her sleep, her ear caught some human voices. She opened her eyes, turned quickly to look, and cocked her head for a better hearing angle. They weren't familiar. She kept low but pulled herself to where she could barely see a group of people, through trees, and stayed as quiet as she could.

# CHAPTER EIGHT

# Catnip

*Grabbing the floor with every muscle in her...*

"And that's why we need to remain just as we are. Defying the corporate structure that's robbed humanity of its soul," came a confident male voice.

"But to what effect? Who cares what we say?" a woman's voice questioned. "We're doing what we like, but how does that create change?"

"People see us. First we look strange, but then they'll start to envy us, want to be like us. Maybe they'll join us or start groups of their own. It doesn't matter."

"You think we're that special?" a different male voice chimed in. "You think we're something that's never happened before?"

"Absolutely not," the first voice came, "absolutely not. We're the hippies, we're the Dadaists, we're the *comedia dell'arte* of the Middle Ages. We're beyond time. We're what shakes humanity out of its rut and returns it to nature, to God."

Another female voice, brusquer, laughed. "So we got an old van, get high when we can, and that makes us Jesus?"

"Yes!" he insisted. "All of them, Jesus, Paul, the Apostles."

"So *you're* Jesus," the other male asked. "I suppose Denise is Mary Magdalene?"

Another male voice, younger, chimed in. "Watch out—that makes you Judas!"

The group laughed. They at least sounded nice, not rough, enough for the dog to relax. This made her start to feel the pain in her legs, so she crept down into some leaves.

The first female turned to the sound. "What's that? Is someone in there? Some kid?"

"I'll check," the younger male offered. "Hello?" He stepped toward the trees. The dog backed up slightly, looking for a way out. "Is there someone...?" He stuck his head in past a bush. She jumped. "*OH*mygod!" he exclaimed as he jumped back.

"What is it?" a woman asked.

"Just a dog. I think it's a shepherd. I just... We surprised each other."

The younger woman stepped up to join him and looked through. "Oh, sweetie," she said when she saw the frightened eyes. "Come on out." She turned to the boy. "She's scared. Let's step away." They backed up. "But come on, honey, it's okay. Won't you come out?"

There wasn't any way to run, and they had seemed nice. The dog took two cautious steps forward, letting just her nose out from the bush. The others laughed. "Come on—it's okay; we won't hurt you," she continued.

With her knees braced to run back, she stepped out

farther, and looked the group over. The woman offered her hand. "Come on…"

The dog sniffed and licked her hand submissively. "Oh, you are a sweetheart, aren't you! Oh my God, your sad eyes! Come on over. Meet the group."

As the dog took two more steps out, the woman introduced them. "I'm Denise. This guy who scared you, he's Clete. Don't worry—he's the nicest of us all. And that tall one, he's Danny. That's Billy, sitting down—I'll bet you heard him talking a lot! And that's Helen over by the—Oh, Helen bring him…" She looked under the dog's legs. "Her…bring her a treat!"

A woman, most of whom was covered in drawings, stepped up slowly and squatted down to the ground, smiling at her. "Would her like a cookie?"

While the dog paused, Danny spoke up. "Isn't it fascinating how we change our grammar for an animal that doesn't understand it in the first place? Using the objective instead of the subjective. Or asking an obedient one, 'Who's a good doggy?!' as though they'd answer."

"Don't listen to him. He's a pompous ass," Helen cooed as she offered a piece of a chocolate chip cookie in her outstretched hand. "Her knows just what I'm saying and is about to be very happy."

"Isn't chocolate supposed to be bad for them?" Billy asked.

"This little bit isn't going to hurt her at all. Is it, sweetie?" Helen continued, coming closer.

The dog kept her legs ready to bolt, but sniffed upward,

and took it out of the woman's hand. With the little under-standing she'd developed about humans, she didn't know how to judge these. Not mean, but not nice in the way the children had been. Just…different. She pulled back toward the trees, and gulped the cookie down quickly, in case they realized how good it was and wanted it back.

Helen walked back to the bag, keeping her smiling eye on the face licking its lips. "Does her want more?"

Clete stepped up to the dog and put his hand out to her. "Would you rather stay here for now?" She licked his fingertips, for the taste more than to show she wasn't a threat, and he reached over to stroke her head slightly.

"Hey, Clete, be careful. She's scared," Denise warned.

"I think she's all right," he said softly, more to himself than in answer.

"She's got a collar—someone owns her," Billy said, get-ting up. "Probably near here. We'd better…"

The dog yelped. Clete pulled his hand back. "I only touched her ear."

"That's what I was warning you about…Oh no…Clete, look."

Clete saw what she meant—the tear in her other ear. "You're hurt, aren't you? Did someone do this to you?" Denise, keeping a few feet away, walked around looking over the dog's body. "Helen, hand her another cookie from over there."

Helen did, and the dog limped toward her. All the people let out moans. "You poor thing," Danny offered. "What are we going to do with you? She doesn't have any tags."

"We can't take her with us," Billy stated. "We can try to find her owner and get her back, if you want. She's probably hurt herself by being out here and needs to get home."

"I can take care of her if we don't," Clete offered.

"Not in my van," Billy said. "That dog'll puke her guts out the first time we get on the road. How old do you think she is?"

Helen rolled her eyes as Clete turned on him. "We all paid for the van, Billy. Stop acting like you're the boss here."

"What! You'd still be in your little bedroom in your parents' bougie house if I hadn't done this. And Danny, don't you give me that look."

"I thought we were against the patriarchy," Danny warned.

"Oh, stop with the words. Yes, you're the one who's been to college, we all know."

"What are you talking about? You went to—"

"Look, man, this is my vision, and I don't need your disrespect!" Billy blurted. He turned and stomped off.

Denise sighed and walked after him.

"Oh, look, she's trembling." Helen squatted down, offering another cookie. "You're not good with all that emotion, are you?"

The dog ate the cookie, more relaxed now that the man's anger had walked away. All of them looked out to see Denise comforting Billy, and then them kissing each other.

Clete turned away from the sight, grimacing, while Helen offered, "Let's get packed up, while it's still light."

They picked up their bags and started loading them into an old van parked on the road.

The dog followed them and sniffed the door, but turned away as they stepped in.

"So what are we gonna do with her?" Danny asked, loading in a guitar.

"I don't know," Clete mumbled. "I don't want to just leave her here." He reached over to pet her, but she backed up, remembering her ear. Annoyed, he reached farther. "Come on, I'm not going to..." She yelped again—was he going to grab her collar?—and ran from him, this time into the van, where she crouched behind a seat.

"Oh no," Billy moaned, walking up. "What the...what do we do now?"

"That's the scaredest dog I've ever seen," Danny smiled. "She's not even a scaredy-cat. She's...catnip! That's what we should call her, Catnip!"

Both the women laughed, and Clete smiled, but Billy winced. "Don't give her a name! We've got to give her *back*!"

"Come on, Catnip! I've got more cookies for you!" Helen offered. The dog started inching toward her and gave a little whine.

"Oh, you are cute, aren't you," Clete cooed. "It's okay." He gave a little whine back at her, to encourage her to come forward.

She looked up at him questioningly. He laughed and imitated her whine again.

She was feeling too much—fear of being pulled out of the van, excitement over the cookie, uncertainty about all these people, and now this? She rolled over, exposing her tummy to Clete and let out a screaming yowl. Clete jumped back in surprise, looking at the others, and laughing "Check this out!"

"Tell you what, Cletie," Billy offered. "You're so attached to her, why don't you take her for a walk and see if you can find her home."

Clete took an annoyed breath but offered his hand to her. "Come on." Everyone stepped away from the door, and she stepped out. "Come on, girl."

He slapped his leg, and the others motioned to her to go. She stood up, shook herself all over, and nervously followed him.

"YOU REALLY SHOULDN'T be afraid of me, you know. I'm sorry about your ear, but it was the other one I touched. I'm a really good person, even if some people prefer other sorts."

He turned and looked at her as they walked. "You don't have the slightest idea what I'm saying, do you? Or do you get it all?"

Catnip didn't answer, just kept walking, unsure of everything, but liking how it reminded her of walking with the boy.

"She's going to dump him sometime. I'm just waiting. But it's amazing—she's so smart in other ways, but falls for his stupid crap every time.

"Of course, so do I. I mean, what am I doing with you here? I don't even want to give you back to whoever...

"Tell you what. Let's wait by this corner and see if anyone comes by who recognizes you. And if they don't, I'll find a way to get them to let you stay."

Clete sat by an intersection, and Catnip lay near him. "Is there any part of you that doesn't hurt?" he asked. "Is my hand scary everywhere?"

He reached over by her, and she rolled over to show him her tummy. "That's a girl! That's my Catnip!" He smiled. He rubbed her chest and tummy softly, and she stuck her tongue out in little licks of comforted gratitude.

A car stopped at the stop sign, the aged driver smiling at them. "Hey, you don't know whose dog this is, do you?" Clete asked.

"Looks to me like she's yours." The lady grinned and drove off. Clete smiled back.

Catnip wandered over to some bushes to sniff around. A large shiny pickup truck drove up. Clete stood and walked up to the window, which lowered electronically. A man in a suit with a crisp new cowboy hat looked out at him. "Really?"

"What?" Clete looked around.

"Get a job, punk."

"Wait, no, I—"

"No?" the man glowered at him. "Gen-Z. I'm so sick of you. Look at you. You're healthy. But you think you're so much better than us. Entitled brats."

Catnip didn't like what she felt from the driver and took a step farther back. Clete's mouth hung halfway open.

"You're even white. Sure, I wouldn't hire a lot of the trash around here either, but don't tell me you can't get a job at 7-Eleven or Jack in the Box."

"I'm sorry, you don't understand, I'm—"

"Oh, I understand. We're sick of taking care of you spoiled kids. When I was your age, my dad had me working in his factory as a manager! He had me firing crud like you, so I'd learn how the world works. And here you expect some handout just for being here. Well, your whole generation can go straight to hell!"

Clete opened his mouth, but before he could think of any words, a noise came from behind him. "Clete?"

He turned to see Helen, followed by Danny, Denise, and Billy. "Is this the owner?"

"Oh, more of you. Look at you, your scruff and tattoos. You all could do just fine. I've seen stories about kids like you, scamming innocent, hard-working, good people. I should call a cop. I'll bet you've got drugs, don't you?"

"What's with you?" Billy asked. "Do you have a problem?"

"Do I have a problem? *Yes*, I have a problem, with you little turds. 'Hey, dude, gimme a dollar, *man*. And benefits!' Well, no, I'm not going to. I pay way too much in taxes, and I give a big donation to my church every year, which goes to the *real* poor, not scum like you."

Denise stepped forward. "Mister, I don't know what's got you so hostile, but no one's asking you for anything."

Danny added, "You know, you're just the sort of creepy cis-gendered male who's been raping this world for the last couple of millennia, and—"

The man's mouth opened in shock. "I don't believe you guys! Look, here's a donation." He turned and grabbed a large coffee cup, ripped the top off, and threw the steaming liquid at them. Catnip jumped back, but the others all were hit in the faces.

"Hey, jerk! You can't do that!" Billy yelled as the truck drove off, with the driver's hand waving a goodbye finger at them as it disappeared.

The group stood in silent shock.

"Geez, Clete," Billy finally spoke. "What'd you say to him?"

They walked back to their van to change their stained shirts. Clete smiled at Catnip and whispered, "At least the jerk ruined Billy's plan to get rid of you!" Her nose sniffed at the younger woman's pocket, hoping for more cookies.

"How much do we have left?" Danny asked Billy.

"Oh, we're good for a few days. Oh, and Denise's aunt just told her she'll put us up in L.A. till we can get our own place, so we're fine. Sorry, should've told you guys before."

"Cool," Danny said. "So as the only legal adult here, I'm going to suggest I get us a bottle of wine. Maybe one for us and another for Clete—I mean, kid, how much of his grotesque bile did you take?"

"I'm sure he has more!" Clete smiled.

"A walking gall bladder," Helen boomed out.

Catnip looked around confused at the laughter. She'd never felt human emotions change so quickly before, not even with children. These folks worried and comforted her in equal measure, but she liked something about them. Something that told her they weren't the sort to deliberately hurt her.

"No, we don't want to rent any theater. Our work needs to be done in the streets," Billy explained as they started their second bottle of strong-smelling liquid. "Damn the locked doors! We want to be among the people, shifting perceptions and opening minds."

"But don't we want them opening their wallets, too?" Helen offered.

"They will. Once they love us. And they will."

Denise looked at him dubiously, but laid her chin upon his shoulder and took his hand in hers. Catnip rolled over in the grass and growled in pleasure at the backscratch it offered. Danny passed her a plate and poured a bit of wine into it. "Danny, that's the third one; you're going to make her sick!" Helen complained, but Clete and Billy just snickered.

"We've got to find where that pooch goes," Billy suddenly muttered, looking accusingly at Clete. "You sure you tried?"

"You saw the response I got," Clete snapped back.

"Well, why don't we walk her and see what we find?" Denise suggested. "It's dark now—maybe her family's home and looking for her."

The others stood up, agreeing. "Which way?" Danny asked. Clete headed off in the opposite direction from where he'd gone earlier, and the rest followed in agreement.

"Do you think we need a permit for street theater?" Denise asked as they headed down their third block.

"I don't know, Denise," Billy responded with some irritation. "But what are they going to do, lock us up?"

"Man, this place feels deserted," Danny said, looking around. "Does everyone go to bed at eight here?"

"Hey, Billy, you could do some theater in the street here and see if anyone comes out," Clete joked, getting just a sneer from Billy. They walked another block, Catnip liking the walk but feeling oddly tired. Then another, with no one coming up with anything more to say.

"Guys, I think we need to just give this up," Danny said. "There's nobody out at all, and I don't want to go knocking on doors."

"Wait!" Billy blurted. "Look!" Just ahead of them was a large house with a driveway holding three vehicles. One of which was a familiar-looking pickup truck.

"Oh, but there must be loads of them here," said Denise. "No way of knowing if it's..."

"Come on, Clete!" Billy motioned. "Is this it?" The two walked up carefully to the side and looked in. Sure enough, there was the cowboy hat and empty coffee cup.

"Whaddya want to do?" Helen smirked. "Ring his doorbell and run off?"

"He deserves better than that," Billy said, thinking. "He's awfully proud, and pride's a deadly sin, you know."

"Yes, Billy," Helen looked at him pointedly. "We know."

Billy, missing her point, looked the truck over. "We could let the air out of his tires, but that's no fun. It needs to be something—"

"I have a better idea: Let's get out of here. Mister Cowboy-wannabe probably has a six-shooter he'd love to try out," Danny whispered.

They stood thinking for a moment. Catnip walked up, sniffed the van, and turned and squatted to pee on it.

Clete looked up. "That's it!"

"What?" Billy asked.

"Credit Catnip. I'll be right back!" He turned and started running back from where they'd come.

"What, you're getting more to drink, so you can...?" But Clete was gone. Billy thought and laughed quietly. "No, a couple of flat tires ought to do the job." He walked up to the back of the truck and pulled out his pocketknife.

"No, Billy, let's just go," Denise begged.

"It'll just be a second," Billy promised, kneeled, and put his knife against a tire.

BRAAAAAAAAM! The truck's horn started blaring and its lights flashing. Billy grabbed his ears and jumped back. Catnip ran into the street in a panic—was it going to attack her like those ones on the road long ago?—while the group scattered. The house door opened, and the man appeared. He pulled out his keys and clicked the button to stop the alarm, and walked up to the front door of the truck, clearly annoyed. He opened it and looked in. "Stupid sensors..."

He grabbed a flashlight and shone it around. None of the people were in sight, but he caught the flash of Catnip's eyes across the street. "Oh, of course. Coyotes..."

He looked around on the ground and found a rock. "Get outta here!" he yelled and threw it at Catnip. She yelped as it hit her leg, just out of fear, as it wasn't strong enough to hurt.

The man turned and ran into his house, slamming the door shut. After a few seconds, the group came back out, one by one. Denise walked over to Catnip. "Good girl!" Catnip didn't respond, unsure of what was coming.

"Get back over here!" Billy whispered loudly.

"No, Billy, we've got to go. He'll come out again," Denise whispered with a new sternness.

"I'll just do it quicker." He headed back to the truck, when Clete appeared behind them, holding a big cardboard box, whispering loudly. "Billy, hold up! This'll be way better."

"What?"

Clete walked to the truck, put the box down, and pulled out a jar of paint. "We've got enough for everyone. Pick a color!"

"No, Clete!" Helen hissed. "You'll set off the alarm again."

"Paint gently!" Clete insisted. "Like this!" He wiped a brushful of yellow onto the back fender.

"What are you doing?!" Danny rasped, grabbing his arm. "This is property damage, vandalism."

"That's what he'll think," Clete grinned, pulling back and standing up. "He won't realize it's body paint, any more than you did."

Danny stood back, impressed. "And it'll rinse off…"

"Whenever he washes it. Or it rains. But not till then." Clete gave a toothy smile and looked the group over. They paused two seconds, thinking, before all ran to grab brushes and jars.

Catnip's curiosity wouldn't let her stay away. The paint smelled interesting, and she could feel the giddy joy of each of the artists as they let their muses run wild over the truck. Clete painted wild florid designs, Helen diamond-like geometric figures. Denise covered a side in a landscape with clouds and birds, Billy adding cartoon characters, while Danny emblazoned the hood with a gorgeous rainbow, with "All love is love" in white along it, and added a turd-emoji figure around the brand logo on the front.

After a couple of minutes, the group stepped back to inspect their work. "If we can paint a set this fast, we're going to be in great shape," Billy acknowledged.

"Wait," Clete muttered, and stepped forward with his brush.

"No, come on, let's get out of here," Denise moaned, though her taking photos of every angle of the truck denied her urgency.

"This is quick," Clete muttered, as he wrote, in huge orange lettering across his earlier design, "DOWN WITH COPS!"

"What, did you have some bad experience or something?" Helen asked.

"Oh, not at all. Didn't you know? Most of my family are police. I figure I might go into forensics work for them someday myself if the acting doesn't work out."

"Well then, why—?" Denise started, as the door to the house flew open, and the man stood, stunned, staring at his newly psychedelic vehicle. The group stood equally still. Till suddenly, "*Go!*" she screamed.

The five sprinted down the street as fast as their legs could. The man threw down his beer bottle and bounded after them. Clete tripped and fell onto the pavement. He looked up to see the man heading toward him, when Danny yelled out, "Hey, Mister!" The man turned as Danny pulled his pants and underwear down, laughing at him.

His moment of shock was just long enough for Clete to pull himself up. The man started after him again, and as they turned into an unlit yard, he reached out, barely touching Clete's shirt, when next to them came an ear-piercing howl.

The man spun to look to the sound. Catnip, sitting stiffly, yowled out in fear and confusion. The man turned to see Clete's body disappear around a corner. He smiled. "Yeah, you kids deal with the coyotes. I'll find you," and walked back to his truck, cussing out his misery as he approached the front, with its sweet loving rainbows, and walked past it into the house.

A few seconds later, he reappeared. "You still there? Get out of here, you dumb coyote!" The flash of two gunshots as the man fired up in the air. "And stay away! I don't kid around!"

A window opened one house down. "Damn you to hell, Brett, get back inside and lock that away or I'm gonna call the cops on you again!"

Brett turned toward the window, but just waved and stormed into his truck, with the gun across his lap.


THE FIVE STOOD, panting, by their van. "I was sure we were goners," Danny breathed.

"At least I was," Clete got out between exhales. "I couldn't tell, what did you do to stop him?"

"Oh, nothing," Danny giggled, as Catnip walked up to them, glad to be away from the angry man with the loud noise. Denise ran to her. "You're amazing!" And the others joined in. All their petting felt good, but it wasn't enough to calm her down. Clete stepped away, to massage his scraped arms and knees.

Helen noticed him, and then exclaimed, "Oh, Clete!" His face had taken some of the fall too, and blood was coming out of the rough red skin. "Let me clean you up." She stepped toward their van, when headlights started to light up the street.

Billy looked up at them, "Wait, that's..." He squinted to make out the vehicle coming, then jumped. "*Into the van! Now!*" The others didn't wait, Danny throwing a yelping Catnip in ahead of him.

Billy turned on the ignition and floored the accelerator. Clete, behind his seat, looked around to where Danny sat in the back. "Do you see anything?" he asked, as Billy turned the wheel hard, knocking everyone to the side.

"Just his lights. What do you think he's trying to do?" Danny yelled.

"Maybe get in front of us and stop us?" Helen suggested.

"Or maybe just scare us?" Denise offered.

The others turned to her. "Did you see what we did to his car?" Billy sneered.

"Okay, okay," she muttered.

"How's my speed, Danny?" Billy yelled back.

"He's getting closer, but I don't think he's trying to cut us off. I'm not sure what—"

A gunshot rang out. "Oh, what the hell!" Billy exclaimed. "Was that at us?" Catnip pulled herself farther under a seat, grabbing the floor with every muscle in her.

Danny shook his head. "I don't think so. He's too close to miss. Maybe it was a warning shot to get us to pull over?"

The box on the dashboard started buzzing. "Oh no, radar," Billy moaned.

"What do we do now?" Denise asked. "We can't…"

"Keep going. Fast," Clete ordered Billy.

"What? We're breaking like five laws here. You want to make it worse?"

"Just do it; trust me," Clete demanded, in a tone no one there had heard out of him before.

"Clete, I've got to…" Billy answered, irritated, as he slowed from ninety miles an hour to sixty.

"When are you going to start *listening?*" Clete roared. He shoved himself over the center console, pushing Billy half off his seat, and stomped the accelerator. The van erupted with screams, while the buzzing of the radar detector grew yet louder.

"Clete, what the hell are you…?" But Billy choked as he saw, out the window, the black-and-white car waiting by the side of the road. "Damn it, Clete! You idiot!"

The police car's headlights flashed on, its flashers and siren started, and it gunned to pull out after them, just as the truck nearly hit it, swerving out and spinning around before continuing after them.

Clete exhaled and pulled himself back over. "Okay, it'll be all right now."

"What are you talking about, man? We're screwed!" Billy barked at him, slowing and pulling over, just in time for the truck and the police car to speed past them, the cops' headlights illuminating Clete's graffiti.

"Oh...right," Billy exhaled as they disappeared into the distance.

"Let's find a place a little more out of the way, why don't we?" Helen suggested, and Billy, nodding, turned off the main road back through some houses.

THE CELEBRATION WENT on for two hours, with cheerful debates about what was worse for the man—speeding, driving drunk, or Clete's art. Catnip curled up outside, feeling safer away from the crowded feet and the boys enjoying giving her more wine. And eventually, contentedly, still not quite sure what to make of the day, she dozed off to the sounds of their happy uncorking of a third bottle.

She slept hard that night—her dreams of the laughter of the young troupe, always interrupted by the fury of the man's gun—which would wake her for a few seconds, till she'd remember where she was and curl up again.

But then, the fourth or fifth time, something felt off. What was it? Was someone approaching?

She opened her eyes and looked around. No, the people were all still in the van. Her head felt dizzy, but she could still see in the light. The light which, as she turned, she could see came from the front of an old pickup. And suddenly hands were on her, grabbing her off the ground before she had a chance to bark, and throwing her in.

And the familiar face smiling at her, as she scrunched down, feeling all hope drain from her heart.

"Hello, Ilse."

# CHAPTER NINE

# Captive

*And just as she rounded the corner, the hit came…*

She crouched down in fear. He reached for her, and she rolled over, showed her belly, and peed a little. "No need for that. Let's go home. You'll be all right." He lifted her into the back seat where she curled up as tightly as she could. He got in front, turned, and shifted the truck into reverse, giving her another glance. "You're looking halfway decent, just a couple of scrapes. Someone musta been feeding you. Oughta give you a brush down, though."

THE OTHER DOGS barked out a huge welcome when they saw her, though she couldn't make out whether the barks were happy or something else. But she felt a desire to be with them, a desire she wasn't used to.

The man pulled her into his house and shut the door. He poured her some food, but she didn't feel hungry. Besides, scavenging and cookies had now set her tastes above his kibble.

While she lay down by the bowl, hoping somehow things would be all right, she heard him talking in the next room. "Yeah, I found her, so how soon can I bring her in? Oh yeah, I can do early. Okay, see you first thing." She then heard a machine turn on loudly, with the sounds of people talking.

He walked in and looked at her. "Damn. It always sets me back when one of you lives out for a while. All the training goes." He opened up the door to the back yard. "Come on. If you don't want to eat, get out there."

She stepped out nervously.

Colt and Needles naturally came to her first, sniffing with interest. She lay on the ground submissively and let them. Colt licked her face, and she liked it, but she was too nervous to return the kiss. The puppy then approached and licked her tummy as before. She looked adoringly at him. Maybe this would be okay.

They stepped away, and she got up to look for the water bowl.

And just as she rounded the corner, the hit came.

Acacia dove in on Ilse's neck from where she'd been waiting. But this time Ilse had expected it. She slammed onto the ground, but rolled herself upright, the hair on her back raised and teeth exposed in a snarl. Acacia went for her neck again, but Ilse ducked and went straight for her left foreleg, biting down as hard as she could.

Acacia screamed, and bit at Ilse's hurt ear, but Ilse still wouldn't let go. Acacia pulled back and tried biting Ilse's shoulder and even her forehead, but Ilse kept in, her head tucked down, till Acacia finally whined and rolled to the ground.

Ilse knew she'd attack her again, but she couldn't stay there forever, so she backed up quickly as she let go. Sure enough, Acacia rose growling, holding her left leg up, but even more ferocious.

Obeying pure instinct, Ilse lunged for Acacia's throat from the side, knocking her to the ground. She knew she could kill her from here, but that wasn't her goal. She just wanted to end the attacks for good. Waiting for Acacia to calm down, just as she'd seen Colt do to Needles, she listened for any signs of submission.

Suddenly a searing pain tore into her back. "*Off*, Ilse!" The man, above, stood holding his belt in the air, yelling, even as she let go and went to the ground. Acacia ran away from both of them.

The man watched her go, put his arm down, started looping the belt back into his pants, and looked back down at the cowering creature beneath him. "Ilse, you did good. Real good. I didn't know you had it in you. Acacia's tough, and you got the best of her.

"Now sure, this time it's probably because she didn't expect anything from you. But now I know what to train you for. You're gonna turn out a better idea than I'd thought."

He turned and walked into the house. Ilse glanced out at the other dogs, who now looked back at her with fear and respect.

This was new for her. She'd been viewed with love, and

with hate and indifference, but not these feelings. It felt uncomfortably new, and oddly secure.

It wasn't what she'd wanted. Now or ever. She'd rather have had playmates or even just companions. But this would have to do. As when she was outside, survival had to come first. Licking her wounds, she curled up into a ball, and, as soon as her eyes grew tired, fell asleep, knowing this time she'd be left alone.

THE NEXT MORNING, the man came out of the house with a leash, put it on her neck, and led her into the car. He drove her back to the place from before, where they poked her more and put some painful medicine onto her ear, and a little bit onto other spots where she'd been cut or bitten. When they asked him about the belt marks, he said they'd happened when she was away from him, that he had no idea who'd done what.

After a short wait, the nice doctor from before came back in. "Neville, we got the test results. Now you can still do this if you want, but you ought to know, she's at five weeks."

The man closed his eyes and mouthed some curses. "Go ahead. It's cheaper than having them. I don't have room, and no one's gonna want 'em."

The doctor took Ilse back through the lobby to another room, filled with cages. She suddenly didn't like this but didn't fight as they put her inside one. Why bother? Was it any better to be out where they stuck things in her, or with the man with the hair on his face? She wanted to feel good again, cared for again, but that was impossible.

She let out a sigh and lay down. At least she might be safer.

After an hour or so, a sweet young woman came to get her. Ilse hoped she'd take her to her home, but all she did was lead her into another room and lift her onto a table. She petted her and told her everything was going to be fine, but then stuck another painful needle into her. Almost instantly, Ilse's eyelids got heavy, and she fell asleep too quickly to even move.

The next thing she knew, she saw tiny bits of light, but everything was spinning, and she wasn't sure of anything, except that she hurt down by her tummy. She wanted to lift her head and lick it but couldn't move anything. After a long time, dozing in and out, things slowed down enough for her to realize she was back in the cage. Still, she barely recognized it. Everything was off.

But there was something else. Something felt very wrong, like when she caught herself breaking a rule. But there weren't any rules. It was just not the way it should be. Like she wasn't who she should be. She couldn't understand it. She just whined and fell back asleep.

The next time she awoke, the nice young woman was opening her cage door and speaking to her lovingly. Ilse lifted her head to sniff her, as she wrapped a huge collar around her neck, so long that it went past her nose. She tried to wriggle out of it but couldn't.

What was this? She couldn't see to the side, all her hearing had an echo to it, and she couldn't get to that pain in her abdomen to lick or chew on it. She whined in imploding frustration. There was no way to turn, nowhere to go. She just had to stay, trapped, with the cone, and the pain, and the cage, and the chance that the man would come back.

And with that something else, that sense of something being off, wrong.

She fell back asleep, the only place she could run and jump and see forever all around her. But the doctor woke her and brought her out, clipped the leash back on her, and led her back to the man. He petted her, and she didn't even pull away. Still too trapped inside. He took her out to his car and carefully lifted her into the back, positioning the cone collar in front of her.

WHEN THEY GOT back to his house, he carried her inside, pushing the dogs away with his foot. He laid her gently on a few towels and patted her. "Just relax, Ilse. Your only job now is to heal."

As before, his voice was so calm, so warm, that Ilse felt comforted and safe and was able to drop off to sleep, though this felt strange to her. It seemed to her that she could trust humans while they spoke in such tones, but it was best to stay aware that their behaviors would change when their tones did.

She woke the next morning to loud voices from a bright machine like the one the girl had liked. The man was walking around the house in shorts and a T-shirt, fixing himself some morning food. "Oh, hey Ilse. Sleep good?" He smiled at her. She gestured a slight submissive tongue out and closed her eyes again and sighed—most likely he wouldn't do anything rough with her if she was so peaceful.

Each morning and night he gave her canned food she liked, taking the cone off for her to eat and for walks outside, where he kept the other dogs away from her, but then tying it back on before she could lick the places she wanted to. In between, he barely spoke to her or anyone else, just sitting in front of the machine, watching and listening to it, or going out to the other dogs. She was glad to be kept in, but wondered what he was doing out there, especially when she'd hear a yelp or his voice raised.

One morning, however, she felt him become more agitated. When he checked her over, as he did every few hours, his touch was rougher. When he poured himself cups of the hot bitter-smelling liquid, he spilled it, and he burned his fingers lighting up a smoking stick.

Eventually he picked up his smaller machine and carefully pressed into it. As he put it to his ear, he sat down nervously, and then looked up at the sound of a voice through it.

"Hello? Hi, Nick? Yeah, it's me, Dad. Neville."

He spoke in a higher tone than Ilse'd heard before, nervous, eager.

"Hey, happy birthday, old man! How're things going?"

He smiled, and nodded at the answers he was getting, with occasional "uh-huh"s that came out more as "ah-hah"s.

"Oh, she is? Oh, that's great. What a girl. And how're..."

He listened more, and let out a laugh, too big. "Oh, Nicky—that's terrific, just great."

And after a pause—"Well? Good, actually! I'm doing fine. Things are mostly the same here, except...Well, I got a new dog. Ilse. She's...You'd like her. Some sort of shepherd mix. She'd be good with Stephanie. You oughta come over and..."

He listened, keeping the smile but with just a little wince. "Oh, that'll be super. Yeah, let me know when works. And are you doing anything special for...Oh, sure, your mom bakes the best cakes, but you know that. And I hear Buck's great with a grill, so that oughta be just..."

He pulled his smile tighter and nodded. "Oh, sure. Hey, great talking to you! Don't do anything I wouldn't, okay? Now you be sure to kiss Marie for me. Promise?"

He laughed another too-hard laugh. "Got it. Will do. See ya!"

He laid the machine on the table and pressed it. He looked down for a moment, but then caught the wide eyes taking him in and turned to face her.

"I wonder how much you mutts pick up. Well, pretty simple, really. You see, I was married once. Yeah, me. Head over heels in love, damned fool. Didn't see what she was till it was too late. After we had Nicky. And how I loved her was nothing compared to—well, I guess every dad thinks his three-year-old kid's the best, but he really was. Funny and smart and just crazy about his dada. And then she left me for Buck and took him with her. And I didn't want to put him through what I had to go through when my folks split, so I didn't fight her. Just saw him when she wanted. And he's turned out fine. I was right, he's better off. But Buck's his dad more'n I am. And we both know it, but we...we pretend.

"See, that what I like about dogs. You don't pretend. 'Cacia's meaner'n a hornet but she's honest.

"And you? I still haven't figured you out. But you showed me a little, and we're gonna find out."

He got up and turned on the bright noisemaker again, sat down to look at it, and lit up another one of his sticks. Ilse didn't move, but just kept watching him, till long after he'd fallen asleep with the light from the machine dancing over his face.

She'd heard more words out of his mouth in ten minutes than the whole week before. And as he was speaking, she saw his sadness, felt his pain. Which made her confusion pull her inside more—maybe she should trust him?

And meanwhile, that other off feeling continued. A yearning she'd never had before—like she was supposed to be with something or someone—but which wasn't there.

THEN, ONE MORNING he led her outside the door, past the other dogs, and into his truck, and took her back to the odd-smelling place. The nice woman carefully took out the metal pieces from her tummy and checked her out, and told him, "She's good to go. Give her a day or two before you run her, but she doesn't need to stay still anymore." Then smiling into her eyes: "It's time to enjoy life again, Ilse!"

For that day, she got to walk around the house, sniff, and—at last!—lick herself. Dogs are much better than people at letting the past go, so she had no problem rejoining life without the cone (though hoping she'd never have to wear one again).

The next morning, the man took her out to train. He started slowly: "Sit," "Stay," "Heel," "Come." And she remembered those reasonably well. So no jerks or clicks, even a few treats—life was good.

When he then left her in the yard, she felt prepared. Any time Acacia or Needles came near her, she snarled, and the other dog slinked away. Even Colt and the puppy gave her more space, intimidated by what they'd seen her do.

THAT NIGHT, THE man let her sleep inside again. She didn't know what she'd done differently from before that would make him so much nicer, but maybe it had something to do with the nice lady and the cone. Whatever it was, clearly everything was going to be all right now.

So even after she had been back outdoors, beyond the little girl's house, and marveled at the splendid landscape all around her, she wasn't too disappointed when she awoke to find she was stuck in a warm home in a fenced-in yard again.

A few hours later, the man took her outside. He went over the lessons from the previous day, and she got them all correct.

He kneeled and scratched her head. "That's really good, Ilse. You're smarter than I'd realized. But today, we're going to start on a new kind of training, girl."

He put a thick clothing over his arm. "Let's see how well you play." He petted her a few times, and then playfully knocked her to the ground, with the arm. She curled up submissively.

"Hmm. That's not going to work. Okay." He got a stick, and shoved it in her face, hoping she'd bite it. But the sight of the stick only frightened her, and she pulled back more.

"Hmmph. Okay, if that doesn't work..." He picked the stick up and threatened her with it. Again she pulled back—why was he mad at her? What had she done? She rolled onto her back to show she was no threat.

"Well if you're going to be a wimp with me, I know who you won't be with." He held her down, called, "Acacia!" and gave a whistle.

The older dog walked around the corner to see what he had in mind. "Acacia, *get* her!" he yelled.

Instantly, the dog flew onto Ilse. Ilse tried to turn herself over in time, but the man kept her down until pulling his hand out.

Acacia bit her on the neck and pulled the skin back. Ilse screamed, but managed to catch Acacia's bad leg in her mouth and shoved her with her paws as hard as she could.

Acacia let go, giving her just the chance to jump up onto her feet and lunge at the larger dog's side. Acacia had expected her to go for the neck, so was caught by surprise. Ilse dug her front teeth into her abdomen, Acacia whirled back, and *now* Ilse went for the throat, forcing her down on the ground in two seconds.

Suddenly the man was on them again, poking Ilse hard with his stick and yelling to let go of each other. Ilse pulled back away, and Acacia ran off around the side of the house.

"Good! Now go for the stick, Ilse! Come on!" The man shoved it into her face again, over and over, to get her to attack. But Ilse, frightened and confused, fell onto her back again, pulling her paws in, blinking fast, praying these attacks would stop.

"God *damn* it! What's it going to take?" he yelled at the terrified mutt, giving a whack to her hips. "Come on!" She pulled inward in pain, feeling her surgery tear.

He punched at her with the stick, over and over, but instead of fighting it, she crawled back to a corner. She wanted to lick the hurt area but sat still, not knowing if that would anger him more.

The man grabbed her by the neck and lifted her into the air, yelling into her face, "What do I have to do? Get angry!"

She yelped, but her mind clenched in terror, making her freeze, unable to move. He threw the limp dog to the ground. "You're useless!" He stormed back into the house.

She lay curled up into a ball, her eyes wide. She'd been wrong; she'd never been less safe. There was no way out, nothing she could do to change this life, this world, this nightmare. She stayed frozen.

The other dogs came around to check her out, but she couldn't react, just curled up tighter, trembling, watching them. Colt sniffed at her with some caring, but the others didn't dare come too close.

She sensed an old feeling, what she'd had with her mother. Her brothers and sisters keeping her from getting all she needed, but she still felt Colt's care, that he might protect her.

And that's when she realized what she couldn't put together before. The feeling she'd had—she was a mother. There weren't any puppies, but she still knew, they were coming, or they had been supposed to come, but she was this different self regardless. She was a caring adult, a protector. She was everything her mother had been to her, even if all she felt was something missing.

She felt dizzy. All of this was too much for her. It made no sense, but she knew it was true. She wanted to sleep but was afraid to; she wanted to run but had nowhere she could go; she wanted to scream but feared that howling would bring out the man and his stick.

As if she'd caused it, the door opened, and the man stepped from the house. He looked at her, disgusted. Colt and Needles and the puppy slinked away, but Acacia stayed by her. The man smiled—the worst smile Ilse had ever seen. "Go on, Acacia, that's right. Go on, get her going!"

Acacia lay down on the ground, looking up at him, not sure what to expect. "I told you, go after her!" he yelled, and picked her up by her wounded foot. Acacia shrieked in pain, and he squeezed tighter to hurt her more.

Suddenly, the part of Ilse that had never lived burst to life in fury. Pushing past Acacia, she flew onto the man and bit down on his arm. He screamed out, dropping Acacia. In a wild primal ecstasy, Ilse dove onto his leg, tearing his pants and tasting fresh blood. He kicked at her as she dodged and went for the other leg. The other dogs barked in wild confusion as she kept after him—an ankle, a thigh—as he turned in quick circles, trying to grab at her neck.

Finally, he got hold of her collar and pulled. She screamed but whipped her head around and chomped down, sinking her teeth just enough into his wrist's underside for him to shriek, drop her, and clutch it in pain. As blood poured out from his hand, he stumbled to the gate and yelled to her, "Get out! Go! Get!"

She ran out the gate. He slammed it behind her, cursing at the other dogs who wanted to follow.

She didn't look back.

She flew past the streets she'd learned, past the houses and barrels she'd taken food from, block after block. Pain searing through her, she didn't care. She just ran.

And when she'd passed all the houses, out into the land without sidewalks or signs, where she'd been abandoned, she slowed down, but she kept walking. Walking deeper and deeper into a world she knew nothing of, insisting on this world she knew nothing of, refusing all she knew.

The fear creeped back up in her. Her old fear of being alone, of having no food or shelter. But she kept walking.

She knew she could starve to death out here or be killed by something she'd never seen. But she kept walking.

At the deepest core of her, one thought spoke. Only one:

That she would never go back there again.

That she would prefer to face anything, any horror.

As she set out into a world where that was likely. Refusing to look back.

She was done.

# CHAPTER TEN

# Artemis

*It was worth a chance. She had nothing left to lose…*

S he awakened with the sunrise. She didn't remember how long she'd slept, or where.

She stretched, every bit of her body in pain. The places the man had hit and kicked her, the surgery wound, the muscles that had run so hard and so long, but none hurt worse than her scraped, worn paws. She licked at them, easing the pain for seconds before they'd burn again, and looked around.

After the sameness of the landscape in the town, here was fascinating. Beyond the bushes she'd slept in, long stretches of light-toned dirt, prickly plants sticking up from it, then stretches of grasses and trees, likely full of little creatures. And in the distance, hills and valleys, nothing she'd ever seen before. Not too bad for now. Or for the rest of her days.

Stretching helped. She couldn't run, but she could lie in different positions and lick herself all over, especially the area where she'd been cut. And after a few hours, she felt better. At least good enough to explore.

She stepped out and started sniffing.

So much information lay around her, so much more than she'd ever sensed before. In people's yards there would be some, even in streets there would be a little, but here was endless history. Who'd lived there, who'd bled there, all the secrets in the soil. The rocks told the oldest stories, the plants the latest developments. But that wasn't what really mattered.

What she cared about was food.

What was out here? Were there those seeds she'd found before? Or other plants? She suspected she wouldn't find freshly deposited leftovers as she had in trash barrels. She also knew she wasn't as fast now, so chasing the animals she couldn't catch before was useless.

She found some grasses, and ate a bit, but they didn't feel right.

She kept walking, stopping occasionally to lick and chew a thorn out of her hurt foot. But her nose pulled up; something smelled strong nearby. She followed the scent and came upon a rat that had been dead a number of days. Covered in bugs, the flesh half eaten away, it didn't smell good, but at least it smelled.

She ate what she could of it, swallowing some of the bugs and wiping others off her face as they crawled out of her mouth. Right away, her stomach started to hurt in rebellion against the rot.

She lay, barely moving, staring out. The fear began to take her over again.

She couldn't go back, where that man would surely find her and beat her. She couldn't trust any people anyway now—the bad ones would hurt her, and the nice ones would leave or let her be taken.

There was nowhere to go, and starving was starting to feel more real. A closer threat.

Something rustled in the grass nearby. She lifted her head. A small squirrel just a couple of feet away from her face jumped in shock and ran off. Her ears cocked quizzically, as that voice, that very old voice, started to speak again.

When she had been still, the squirrel hadn't known she was there. If she could be patient and not move a muscle, but keep watch, might that mean she could eat?

It was worth a chance. She had nothing left to lose.

She curled up so that her eyes barely peeked over her legs, and waited. Time went by.

A young squirrel—maybe the same one?—hopped nearby. He stopped to dig something out of the ground. She held her breath, but he left without coming close enough.

Later, a bird stepped near her, but she knew they'd be even harder to catch, so she stayed motionless.

A mouse scurried by. Too fast to catch, and probably too small for the effort.

A fly buzzed curiously, almost lighting on her face. She snapped at it, but it dodged her. But when it returned, irritating her ears, she turned and caught it. She couldn't even feel whether she'd swallowed it or not, but at least she'd stopped the noise.

She sighed and laid her head back on the ground.

Her eyes shut. Fighting the hopelessness.

After what seemed just seconds, she heard another sound. Something stepping nearby. She started to look but thought better of it—and kept her eyes shut.

She inhaled quietly. Whatever it was, it was close. Maybe close enough. She waited for another step. It came. Closer. She waited. Another two steps. Close enough?

She turned and lunged. The squirrel was so surprised it froze in shock, and she was on it before it had a chance to move. She grabbed its body in her mouth and, as her ancestors had for ten thousand generations, before it could turn to bite her, thrashed her head, painlessly breaking its neck.

It went limp, its eyes still shining but its face empty of expression. And for the first time in her life, she ate prey.

It didn't taste as good as the food she'd gotten from humans. But so much better than the half-rotted rat.

And yet, greater than the taste were two sensations—the glory that she'd hunted successfully, and the relief, the hope.

She could do this. Maybe she could survive.

She wasn't weak anymore; she was a huntress, a predator. She'd succeeded and would only become better.

Life was new again.

She slept. The squirrel didn't fill her stomach, but the relief had allowed her to feel the exhaustion in her body. And in her dreams, for the first time, came not memories or fantasies or visions, but thoughts. Her mind tried to work its way around what she'd just done.

This squirrel was some sort of creature. Like the birds, like people, like other dogs. But something stopped when she shook it. What happened to that something? It stopped biting her, which she liked, but where did the part of the squirrel that bit go? That energy. Did she eat it, or did it just stop existing, like a sound?

And if this could happen to a squirrel, could such a thing ever happen to her? Could she similarly just stop? And while the idea seemed incomprehensible to her, something inside said she could, and had in the past, long before this self. And at this, her mind couldn't handle the concept anymore, and she yelped herself awake.

She looked around, feeling more exhausted from the thoughts now than before she'd dozed off. She sniffed and listened. No new beings seemed near. Her eyelids grew heavy, and almost instantly she was out again—but this time with her mind quiet.

After an hour, she awoke and took a short exploring walk, making sure anything she did that left a scent was far away from her den, so there'd be no warning odor to potential food. She walked back and lay down again, waiting for another sound.

This time she didn't drift off. And again, her patience

rewarded her, as a rustle came. She waited, thrust at it—but this squirrel raced to the nearest tree in time.

Twice more that morning, the same thing.

And a new idea arose.

She lay quiet again till she heard the sound, kept low, waiting just long enough, and then leaped up, but this time raced past the squirrel, toward the tree. The squirrel, who'd long ago learned to react to attackers by running for trunks, was more shocked than frightened as her mouth clamped down on it from the side.

By the time she went to sleep that night, the sunset bathing the hillsides in changing tones, she'd caught and eaten three squirrels this way. Her belly full, she felt her energy returning. She wondered if this was what happened with the squirrel's life energy. Had she taken it into herself?

And while she thought, she also realized that all her lying still was helping her body heal from the beatings. She sighed in contentment—after expecting the worst, this wasn't even bad.

But neither, she thought, was the squirrels' lot. The ones she killed. If she was right, if their lives went into hers, they weren't feeling pain anymore, and they certainly weren't being beaten or left by anyone.

What she was living now felt better than being dead like them, she was sure. Life meant victory. But to her, even death would be better than going back into the world of the humans. This was as good as existence could possibly get.

She curled up again in her den and slept with a deeper sense of security, dreaming of triumphant chases and catches.

THE NEXT DAY, she ventured out farther, and saw something like a squirrel but larger, without the long tail and with tall ears. She approached it, when suddenly it jumped and hopped away from her. She gave chase, bounding after it, but it changed direction with each hop. For two hours, although she often whined as he'd whip away from her with a hairpin turn, she was filled with more elation than frustration. As when chasing children so long ago, the running made her head light and the world brighter.

Finally, exhausted, she gave up and wandered away. But some time later, a sound behind her made her turn to see the creature, *that* creature, hopping away contented in its safety, not realizing it was in her direction. She spun after it, knowing that if she closed in, it would turn. So she took a chance, and at the last second, veered to her left. The animal's choice of direction proved its last.

THAT NIGHT, THE sky did what it hardly ever did in those days, let loose some rain. She huddled under her hiding bush but found that she liked the feel of the drops rolling onto her fur, soaking her, cooling her, and easing her scraped footpads. So she lay out in the moisture for hours, unable to sleep, fascinated by how it changed all she saw.

As the sky cleared and the sun arose, so did she. She walked her usual area, loving the mud's feel. Her nose went wild, as the wet now fully released the passionate odors of nature surrounding. She sat to take it all in, when a small bird lighted on the ground beside her. She cocked her head—did the bird not realize she was there?

She pounced. For the hardest animal to catch, this one was awfully easy. Something must have been wrong with it. But still, she walked a bit taller. Able to catch any sort of prey she wanted. She was the queen of the field.

This, she realized deeply inside, was her true self, her essence. Living in the human world offered comfort and easy food, but this was more right. The life she was born for.

Then, suddenly, she felt something she hadn't since she'd found the field. She stopped.

She was being watched.

Was it a human? It didn't feel that way...

Her eyes peeled the landscape around her. Her nose twitched—hard to pick a single smell out of the morning symphony.

And then she caught it. Not even hiding. Just standing a distance away. A grey dog. Skinnier than her, hungrier.

She thought to turn and run but remembered that squirrels and rabbits do just that, so she'd be inviting a chase. Slowly she walked toward it, her head down, shoulders high. The stranger just stared at her.

She didn't like it. This dog wasn't like others she'd known. She barked out of disturbance—something was wrong.

The grey dog started to turn away, then hesitated.

She growled. Still it didn't move.

She crept closer, and closer. The two staring each other in the eyes.

She crouched in the grass. Her hair stood up on her back. She showed her fangs and let out a snarl.

The stranger took one step toward her. She lunged, and he turned and ran. She chased him for a few yards, but then let him go.

She shook herself off, turned back, and headed home toward her bush, across her field, surveying all around her. She looked back. No, he wasn't there.

She barked—half to make sure he was gone, but also wondering if she'd just chased off a playmate, a companion, a fellow hunter.

But when she got no response, she knew. It was for the best. And she had triumphed.

Her chest filled out. The runt that not even her puppy brothers and sisters took seriously was the queen huntress.

And, for all she could tell, her reign would be permanent.

# CHAPTER ELEVEN

# Ares

*So none heard the other sound coming...*

The setting sun shot through the remaining clouds, blasting hues across the rolling hills and fields of shifting golds and deep blues and reds. The slight breeze gave just enough movement to the trees and grasses that even the limited-color vision of the dog's eyes caught the view's majesty.

Content with the day, but ready for it to end, she returned to her hidden spot, pulled some grasses and leaves in to cover the exposed mud, and walked around it three times before curling up upright. She took a deep breath and let the feeling fill her as she looked about her. She didn't bother lying out of sight; she just wanted to relax, lick and nibble her feet, and watch her majestic world darken.

And for the first time ever, she took notice of the little lights in the night sky. She'd seen them before, but were they somewhere else she could go? Somewhere she might have been?

Then, before she fell into oblivion, she sensed something wrong. She looked around, sniffed, twitched her ears in different directions...Nothing revealed itself. But still, again, there was a different energy out there, one not kind.

She focused on it as long as she could, before her eyes drooped down and took her away.

It wasn't dawn yet when they opened again. This time, she heard it. Steps around her, and not birds or mice or squirrels or rabbits.

Bigger.

She held herself still, as for hunting, but out of, not hope, but fear.

The steps continued. It was more than just one creature walking. Two or three at least.

One growled.

Could it be dogs? It couldn't be Colt and Needles looking for her, could it? Or Acacia?

A cloud moved just enough for a little moonlight to shine down, and she was able to make out the skinny body, the matted hair, of the grey dog from this afternoon.

But was it? Something about it wasn't the same. And then she saw why, and chilled.

Another walked by. She watched it. And then, slowly, her ears turned as she heard more sounds behind her. Barely moving her head, she looked—there were more. Lots more. Six, seven, all sniffing around. Were they looking for food? Or for her? She pulled her head down, her heart racing, eyes wide behind leaves.

Could they smell her? Probably not, because of the odors the rain had brought out around her.

Most were the same size as the one she'd seen before, but then she saw one was larger. He stepped with more sureness than the others, and whenever one would step too close to him, he'd turn and snap at them. Was he the leader? Somehow, she felt not. Leaders help their pack, while this one was against the group, although he was one of them.

One looked right at her, through the leaves. She looked away so it wouldn't see her eyes, but still it barked out. She tensed. The others walked toward it, as the large one pushed forward, shoving the discoverer out of his way. But from behind, the one that had seen her bit the big one, who yelped and spun around.

The two stared each other down, snarling. Each stepped slightly to the side, their unblinking eyes locked.

She couldn't see who did what first, but suddenly they were on each other, teeth and claws going full-bore. The others ran barking in high-pitched excitement. She turned to see if she could get away, but some were too close not to see her escape.

She could tell—this fight had been coming from long before this, and it would end only one way. The question was who would stay on top. The smaller one attacked fiercely, scratching at the big one's nose with his claws while biting down on his neck. But the big one had the weight and size to throw him down and rip into his eye. The smaller screamed and pulled back, which gave the larger the moment he needed, and he dove down onto his opponent's throat, grabbing it in his jaws and shaking him like a rodent. The smaller one's eyes rolled up, his body going limp. The larger dropped him down, satisfied.

He turned and looked at the others, as if daring any to try as well.

But the smaller one suddenly sprung, surprising him from behind, pulling onto the top of his back and biting down on the base of his skull. The larger one howled out in pain, writhing, but couldn't get him off him. The smaller kept biting till he ripped into a shoulder muscle. The larger one fell to the ground, while the smaller kept at him.

Finally, the larger rolled over onto his side, beaten. The smaller stood over him in triumph and howled, but that was all the strength he had had left. He fell off his opponent and onto the ground, blood gushing from his eye and throat.

Their fellow pack members, who'd been waiting for a victor to be determined, flew into a frenzy, and fell onto both bodies, loudly finishing them off.

Crazed by the fight, and by the taste of blood in their mouths, they then went at each other. But as none was now the leader, no one knew who to attack. The fighting turned to group howling, a collective madness, and woe betide any creature passing them by in this state.

She decided this must be the best moment possible. She backed herself up slowly, trying to maintain silence, but the leaves she'd brought into her sleeping area rustled just enough for one of them to look up and see her slipping away.

Without a moment's hesitation, it jumped after her

and into the bushes, screaming an alarm. The pack turned from each other to look. What was she chasing? But they charged after her anyway.

The dog turned and ran as hard as she could, her ears folded back, pushing into the dark branches. Struggling to see, she weaved through bushes and trees to lose the attacker, but she didn't know where to head. She ducked behind one tree and then wound around another, but could hear the pack closing in.

It seemed to be heading to her right, so she turned left, skidding so hard she fell onto her side. Instantly, the one who'd seen her was on her. It tried to climb on top of her, but she turned and bit it in the side as hard as she could. The attacker yelped and fell to the ground. She jumped up and kept running, weaving every chance she got, not noticing that the sky was beginning to lighten.

She found an open spot and ran as hard as she could through it, to another clump of trees. Just as she reached it, she turned and looked back to see ten of them sprinting after her. She ran into the woods and weaved as much as she could—through one stand and then another, till she saw another open space, this one larger, and more visible. Instinctively she ran for it, knowing it was her freedom from the attackers—but once she broke through into it, she realized her mistake.

She was in a field.

No longer was she invisible, no more could she weave away from them. She and her world were suddenly naked. Now there was simply one question—could she get across it before they got to her? Her body straining for breath, she tried again to speed up.

But her mistake was too much. The pack spread out, so that wherever she turned there was one on her tail. And they were gaining on her. Closer, closer.

One got onto her left and lunged onto her. She fell to the ground and rolled over, pushing him off. She spun around and tried to attack him, but he bit down into her back. She screamed in pain and threw herself down onto him to loosen his grip.

He let go, and she stabbed her teeth at his chest, biting as hard as she could. He pushed his paws into her, trying to shove her away, but she held on, making him shriek, trying desperately to bite her but only able to get to the top of her head.

She expected the others to jump on her as well, but realized now that they were watching, just as they had their earlier fight.

He twisted himself and bit her right foreleg, trying to crush the bone. She yowled and went for his throat. He fell to the ground, aware she could kill him immediately. They went still. She knew—if she killed him, the rest would fall onto her in a second. But if she let him go, he would come at her harder than before.

A memory flashed in her. Of two other dogs. Of strategy and force. *That might work*, she thought.

She loosened her grip. The enemy waited and then gave a jerk to turn himself around and attack again.

But this was just what she'd planned. She grabbed him by the top of the neck, pulled all her strength to lift him up off the ground, and ran, full speed, into the rest of them, using him as a shield, knocking two back in surprise. They turned and lunged—

And missed her. She dropped him, letting them grab him instead by mistake, and wheeled around. As the trapped predator let out a shriek of terror, she turned and ran.

As hard as she could, she fled into and through the trees, but suddenly the ground wasn't there beneath her feet. She tripped and fell, tumbling onto much harder ground.

In one second, the pack closed in and fell onto her. Paws and teeth ripping into her sides, her face. She screamed and struggled against them, but it was over. There was nothing she could do. Except to take as many of them with her as she could.

She kicked and bit and twisted and pushed, but every movement only brought them in more—biting at her shoulders, her tail, her legs, her throat. Pain seared through every part of her, horror burning at her core.

She howled at the top of her voice, while the vicious attackers barked in glee, so none heard the other sound coming.

The sound that got louder.

The sound that came with light.

The roar. The screaming giant.

They jumped up to run, but with a loud screech, it was too late. Two of them were hit by the swerving beast as it screeched sideways. One got pulled under a wheel, flattened, while she heard another's leg break from the impact.

Barking out, the rest fled in different directions, terrified.

The truck stopped. She looked up. Two men climbed out, one of them colorless in shock saying over and over that he didn't see the coyotes till it was too late. "But wait, what's that other one?"

With everything she had left in her, she pulled herself up and started to walk away.

One of the men ran up to her. "Hey, pup, we gotta get you to a vet." She turned and snarled. He stopped, but squatted down, and put out his hand.

She barked and snapped at it. He pulled it back, her teeth marks in it beginning to bleed, and she turned and pulled herself away. "Sorry, man, she's done for. I can't get her," he yelled to his companion, who was checking out the two coyotes he'd hit.

She limped up the curb she'd tripped over and back into the woods. For the first time tonight, she knew where she was heading.

Just as infinite dogs and wolves had for millennia.

To find a protected spot, a den, where she'd be covered. Where she'd be safe.

Where she could rest.

Where she could die.

CHAPTER TWELVE

# Athena

*Life meant that...*

She awoke. The sun was high. But she didn't know if she'd been there one night or three. She sat up slowly. Everything on her surface burned, and everything inside ached.

She licked herself all over, cleaning off the dried blood as well as she could, before trying to stand. She limped carefully toward a tree, where she slowly and painfully relieved herself. She started to head back to the den she'd found in some rocks, but her thirst won out and she looked around to see if she could find any water.

Fifty paces away, a puddle hadn't dried completely since the rain. She drank it all, and flopped to the ground, her torn body needing a rest from having walked for five minutes.

There was no way she could hunt. But maybe if she could walk some more, she'd find something she could eat.

Sure enough, sniffing found her a half-eaten field mouse, probably dropped by a bird, and some seeds that smelled acceptable. This was enough for now. Her pain wouldn't even let her shake herself after eating them, though her instincts urged her to.

She hobbled back to her den and slept hard again.


AFTER A LONG time out cold, she came to, realizing she had been dreaming about the coyotes returning, and the terror had pulled her out of the dream into a vague reality. She braced herself to shake her body into the day.

But the sounds of their steps continued. Her heart stopped. They were back.

She froze in fear and twisted her eyes to the side to see as much as possible without moving a muscle.

It wasn't coyotes. Worse—it was people.

A man and a woman, just far enough away for her to be safe if she kept quiet, were picking plants and discussing them. She kept down, out of their sight, but she could tell she didn't know them. They kept talking, occasionally laughing. Every now and then, one would give the other a quick kiss.

They sat down to eat. Her nose started twitching, wondering if they might leave any of what they didn't finish. But she kept still. Long enough to fall asleep.

She was startled awake by the sound of scurrying. Very close. She opened her eyes and looked to the side. She could barely make out a possum, eating a seed it had found. Just close enough that she might be able to...

She dove, the possum jumped, and the woman screamed. The dog stopped and looked out—the couple had never moved; they were still where they'd sat. She turned and ran back into the hidden area, hoping they hadn't noticed her, and watched to see what they did.

"I don't know who was more scared, me or the dog!"

"Well, the dog didn't scream."

She giggled and lightly hit the man. "Did it have a collar?"

"I don't know. I'll go get it." The man walked up to where she'd been. "Here, puppy. Come on, pup. I won't hurt you…"

She sat perfectly still. Just as when with bloodthirsty coyotes, she was too smart to move a muscle. She'd learned.

The man wandered around the area but gave up and walked back to the woman. "It must have run off."

She waited for over an hour while they finished their food and left. Only then did she dare to step out.

She walked over to where they'd been and sniffed around. She could smell them and what they'd eaten. But they hadn't left a crumb.

She headed farther, watching to make sure they weren't around, thinking that maybe she'd be able to hunt a little, as long as she was careful to make sure anything she pursued was even closer to her than usual.

THE NEXT MORNING, after another long sleep, she felt a bit better—still limping, but her wounds were healing again. She walked out into the field and gazed around.

For the first time since the attack, she thought of what was coming. She'd known innately that she was dying, but somehow, she was still alive. And maybe she could stay that way, if she could just avoid humans and coyotes. And she liked it here, maybe more than the field she'd had before. Especially as this one had more smell of mice. She wasn't quick enough for squirrels and rabbits now, but mice weren't as smart, so they were perfect.

She jumped after one and caught it on the first try. She found a comfortable spot to lie in the sun and wait, and sure enough, a few minutes later, another mouse ran through grasses too tall for it to see her looming nearby, and quickly paid the highest price for that unawareness.

She lay down to lick herself in glee, but heard a sound in the distance. Footsteps again. She looked.

The same people as yesterday. Pointing at her, moving toward her. She turned and ran, hiding behind a tree. But they were too clever and could tell just where she was.

The woman kneeled on the ground. "Come on, girl. We're your friends. We won't hurt you."

"Here," the man whispered to the woman, and handed her a bag.

"We have goodies for you!" she said cheerfully. "Wouldn't you like a treat?"

"Yummy yummies!" the man called seductively.

"Yummy *yummies?!*" The woman turned and asked him. "Really?"

"Come on, girl!" the man called, laughing. "They're fake meat. You can call them anything you like."

"Sure, yummy yummies!" the woman called to her.

But the dog knew better and stayed still, ready to bolt if they came closer.

The two looked at each other and stood up. "It's okay, sweetie," the woman called to her.

The man put his arm around her, and they walked away. "What do you think happened to her?" the woman asked him.

She waited. Even a squirrel starting down from the tree didn't get her to move. But once they had been gone long enough, she stepped out. She explored, and found, where the couple had been, a pile of savory pellets. She devoured them instantly and sniffed around, licking the ground for any remnants.

THAT NIGHT, SHE slept in a different area, afraid the humans had learned her old hiding places too well. But the next morning, as she ventured out, there they were again. And again, they let her hide, but kept calling to her.

This time, they made sure she saw them leave some more treats, the man smiling. "You know, we watched you eat these yesterday and you seemed to like them! If you come with us, we'll give you lots." But once again, she waited for them to be gone.

She wasn't safe. These people were after her. And they might take her from her field and leave her alone somewhere not as good. Or, for all she knew, they might give her back to the hairy-faced man. She had to find how to get away to where they wouldn't find her.

She didn't know what was what direction but figured uphill would be best. She headed toward a rocky crag and started up. When her legs complained too much, she lay down for a rest and turned around to see where she'd been. But her ears shot up—the couple was behind her! They'd followed her this whole time.

She looked around. There was nowhere to hide nearby. She froze in fear, trapped.

The man walked up to her, very slowly, holding out treats. He spoke in a soft, calm voice, just the way that other man had talked with her in his truck. "It's okay, girl. It's all okay. We're your friends. Can't you take a treat from me?"

She stared, her ears back, eyes wide.

He got closer and reached the treats out toward her nose. "That's a good girl...That's right..."

She barked out and snapped at his hand. He pulled back quickly. "Oh, sorry!"

She growled more. The woman stepped up behind him.

"It's okay. She's just scared," he told her. "She wasn't trying to hurt me. This poor thing has been through hell."

"What did that to her?"

"Some wild animal, I'd guess. Bobcat? Must've been a crazy fight."

The dog looked between them, growling, hoping they were no worse than they seemed. Their smell was nice, their energy seemed nice...but she'd learned better than to trust that.

The woman started to reach out her hand. "Don't," the man said. "Let her..."

"Okay," she said. "It's all right, girl. Take your time."

The two of them turned and walked away.

"Oh, wait," the woman said. She turned back toward the dog. "Here you go." And dumped out more treats.

The dog stayed still but couldn't keep her ears from flashing up for a quick moment, before folding back in fear again.

"Did you see that?" The man smiled. The woman gave a little laugh and they walked away.

"Bye, puppy. Enjoy your meal!" the woman sang softly without turning around.

The dog sat in confusion. Hiding was useless. These people were smarter than coyotes. They could figure out what she'd do, where she'd go. But as long as she protected herself, she might get treats while they did.

She waited for them to be gone, gobbled the treats while looking around to make sure she was alone, and headed up the hill. Then, unable to find a hiding spot good enough, she turned back to the den she'd spent days in, what now seemed so very long ago.

THAT NIGHT SHE dreamed madly. The first man and woman and the girl were there, tossing her out of their car. The other family, looking out the window at her but not helping as she yelped to be saved. The odd youngsters, laughing at her. And the sad man with his stick, approaching with

Acacia and the pack of coyotes, and even Needles and Colt and the puppy, all surrounding her, closing in for an attack, fangs bared and bloody.

She awoke. The sun was just starting up. She stepped out of her den and walked around the field. She could smell where some mice had just been, but couldn't find any.

She kept sniffing and came upon one of those people's treats. She ate it and realized there was another nearby. And then another. She kept eating them, till she saw the couple, lying on the ground, wrapped up in something. She stepped forward with a sniff, to see if they were alive.

The woman's eyes opened, and she looked at her and smiled. "Good morning, cutie!" The dog stood still, ready to run.

The man, with his eyes still closed, pulled closer to her. "Morning…" he mumbled.

"No, not you, dummy, her!"

He opened his eyes, looked at the dog, and smiled. "Hey, pooch!"

The dog didn't know what to do. She sat her haunches down and kept looking at them. Who were they? Did people live in the field with her now?

They kept looking at her, too. Finally, the man turned and picked up a familiar-looking bag.

"We've got more of these," he smiled. "You want some breakfast?" He opened the bag and pulled out a treat to show her.

She barked angrily—would he stop trying to do this?—and turned and ran back into the bushes.

The couple both groaned. "Why are you putting us through this?" the woman called to her.

They got out of their thick wrapping and stretched out.

"Let's go up. We have to try," the man said.

"Sure. Now or never," the woman moaned as she picked up some food and, the dog saw in terror…a leash.

She looked around. She could run, but could she make it? There was no question now—they wanted to take her. And they were a lot bigger than she was, so if they got to her they could leash her, even if she bit them.

The couple approached and squatted down just far enough away from her.

"You know, we can see you in there," the man said.

"Yes, we see your beautiful eyes," said the woman.

"We don't want to hurt you," he said. "We're here to help you. To get you to a doctor. And find you a home. Don't you want a home?"

"Whatever did that to you, it'll happen again. We want to protect you," the woman begged. "We'll make sure you'll have a good place."

The dog looked around. She would have to run so far that they would never find her. As she had so many times before. She'd just gotten lazy, letting them figure out her area. If she worked at it, she could get away.

But she had been safe here, except for them. Were the coyotes out there beyond? She couldn't count on a truck showing up out of nowhere again.

But the worst the coyotes could do would be to kill her.

"Just give us a chance. We promise it'll be okay," the man said.

"You've just got to come out," the woman said, choking up. "Or you're going to get killed, you goofhead."

One of the dog's pulled-back ears perked up. What had she just heard?

The woman wiped her eyes and sniffled. "Sorry," she muttered to the man. "It's just…" She looked up at the dog again. "Come *out!* Would you?"

And in the deep canine eyes, came the view of a little girl's smile. And on her forehead, she felt the soft touch of a small hand. And the nuzzle of a pressed kiss.

The man put his arm around the woman, as she began to weep. "It'll be okay; we'll get her somehow," he promised.

The dog stared at them. The way they treated each other. She had been treated like that. But it always went bad. She was always left, or they turned on her, or…

"Come *on*, you goof!" the woman urged.

Again, she sensed the child. Remembering that acrid odor the girl always bore after walking home from school. When she'd get hugged too tight and her whole world would explode in joy.

That little girl who turned cold to her, whose father yelled and threw her in fury, whose mother drove off in the car.

"Puppy, come on. We're not leaving without you!" the man urged, smiling.

His eyes were so kind. And his outstretched hand, the one she'd snapped at, was there again. And again holding the food she needed.

But she felt another need too. A need she hadn't felt since she could even remember. A hole inside her, a need she'd known in her crate, and in her yard when the family was away. A searing pain of loneliness, a need for someone, that someone.

And she realized that, no longer would she rather die.
   Now, she'd rather live.

If she didn't run away right now, she risked being hit again. Or being caressed.
   She risked being grabbed and thrown—or hugged.
   She risked being hated or loved, being abandoned or protected, having to let someone in or fight someone who wanted to kill her.

Life meant that. Life meant wanting to live. And wanting to live meant...

Terrified, she carefully stepped out from the bushes. She paused and inhaled, to feel all of being, every bit of pain in her. Carefully she slightly shook her shoulders, just as much as she could bear.

And then, one slow step at a time. Her ears wavering back, her nose ahead.

Sniffing for what the outstretched hand might hold.

A couple of years ago, I adopted a rescue dog, a sweet adult German shepherd mix. Silly and friendly—until her previous family left her at my house. Instantly she fell into fear. Fear of my home, and especially fear of me.

I knew a little of her past—that she'd been registered at two homes in the Inland Empire, and that when reached (through data on a chip), each strangely said, "Oh yeah, we had that dog. We just didn't like her much, so we let her go." And that she'd been found in a field, so terrified it took days to get near her.

But she soon told me more: Her fears of certain sounds, of rushing water, of men with beards, of my expressing any strong emotions. Her funny pained howling when annoyed, her excellent hunting skills—and worst, her reaction when I first told her "no"—hitting the ground on her back, her paws pulled in, rapidly blinking...This pup had been beaten, and badly.

For a year, I tried to teach her to trust me and enjoy her life. At times, she would warm up to me, but then sleep roughly and awaken frightened again, apparently having relived experiences in her dreams that kept her leery.

And so I questioned. A DNA test explained her looks. But what had created all these fears and oddities? Why did she treat the only toy she liked in a maternal manner, while shunning real puppies? Why did she enjoy being petted, but scream and snap if someone caressed the back of her neck? Why did she whine into a howl, especially if I joined in with her, whenever I'd arrive home?

I learned what to avoid, what to tolerate, and what to beg forgiveness for. And I began to come up with some answers. Either through imagination—a series of guesses that fit all I'd seen—or by her magically telling me all her memories, I'll never know.

And eventually these ideas coalesced, enough to forge a story. A fictional biography. While at the same time, this mythmaking transformed my view of this dog—from victim to heroine, and from burden to teacher.

THIS BOOK IS dedicated twofold. First, to Tom and Catherine Peters—the saviors who sold her to me, after caring for her for months—and to all the brave and devoted animal rescuers out there, dedicating their lives to our natural betters.

But, even more, to this now joyous angel who has raised my life into another level of understanding. Who likely had

at least five names before I got her. But who has taught me how to see her—as not a past but a vibrant present and future, and as not a martyr but a magical spirit carrying a hidden song.

The most glorious sort of song, filled with emotion, with range, with epic grandeur.


THIS GOES TO the one I call Aria. Who shall remain of that name, now, forever.

## Acknowledgments

A few quick nods for those who've helped bring this work to fruition. To Marie Strauss, who pulled the story back from my too-horrific imagination. To Steven Lowy, lawyer and friend extraordinaire. To Karman Kruschke, whose photographs always capture more of me than I know exists. To Kaiden Krepela, artiste of skills only explainable by her lineage. And to Marissa Eigenbrood, champion publicist for *The Teachings of Shirelle*, who continued her gift by referring me to the great folks at Mindbuck Media Book Publicity.

To all my BFFs at Circuit Breaker Books and Mindbuck Media—Jessie Glenn and compadres Vinnie Kinsella and Deborah Jayne, social media magnate Hannah Richards (who has somehow recreated me online as a much nicer person), highly tolerant web designer Bryn Kristi, and publicist Kristen Ludwigsen (who tirelessly champions this mongrel beast with humor and affection).

And, last but not least, to editors Ali Shaw, Kristin Thiel, and Laura Garwood, who pored through every word to perform interventions on my work; and Lisa Pegram and Mari Moneymaker, who cleaned up my instances of blindness and ignorance; and Mary Cohen, who helped convert my book-learned Spanish to real-*gente* talk.

Books usually list one author on the title page. Thanks to all who made that a lie here.

## Share Your Thoughts

Did you enjoy *A Dog of Many Names*? Then please consider leaving a review on Goodreads, your personal blog, or wherever readers can be found. At Circuit Breaker Books, we value your opinion and appreciate when you share our books with others.

Go to circuitbreakerbooks.com for news and giveaways.

Douglas Green is the author of the widely-acclaimed 2015 book *The Teachings of Shirelle: Life Lessons from a Divine Knucklehead* and runs the advice website AskShirelle. com, based on the wisdom in the book, which he was taught by his ridiculous dog. Having directed the film *The Hiding Place*, he got released from decades in the entertainment business for good behavior, and now works as a psychotherapist in Los Angeles, specializing in children and teenagers.

CPSIA information can be obtained
at www.ICGtesting.com
Printed in the USA
LVHW091457260721
693699LV00004B/212